Requiem for the Caged

By
R.W.K. Clark

This is a work of fiction. All names, characters, locales, and incidents are the product of the author's imagination and any resemblance to actual people, places or events is coincidental or fictionalized.
Published in the United States by Clarkltd.
Po Box 45313 Rio Rancho, NM 87174
info@clarkltd.com

Edition 1
United States Copyright Office
1-5997225634 November 2017
Library of Congress Control Number: 2017919790
International Standard Book Numbers
ISBN-10: 1948312026
ISBN-13: 978-1948312028
ASIN: B078R71DFQ

/200801

CONTENTS

ACKNOWLEDGMENTS

I dedicate this novel to my wonderful readers and for all the amazing people I've met and those I haven't. To my family and loved ones, all your support will not be forgotten.

This book was made possible by reviews from readers like you.

Thank you

PROLOGUE

Darkness can be a dangerous thing, especially when one is kept in it for so, so long.

He had no idea how long he had been there; he had no window to look out of to see the sun or the moon. In the beginning, he had tried to distinguish the time by the sounds and voices that seemed to be coming from all around him, but there was always someone awake there, always some kind of talking. Sleep was not a luxury that could be afforded when there was a war going on.

He knew only one thing for sure: he was in Syria. Initially, when he was first deployed, he was sent to Afghanistan to serve as a medic for the United States Army. He had been afraid; after all, it was a full-blown war he would be in, even though he would not be on the front lines. He had buried his fear and set his face like stone; he didn't have time to whine or tremble because he was a man, and there was a war to fight. His mother had sobbed and begged him to stay, pleaded with him because she was sick and scared. But he had reassured her and went, just as he had sworn to do when he enlisted.

His left hand throbbed unbearably, but he closed his eyes against the pain. His captors had crushed it between two rocks, but not to make him talk. No, they had done it because they were bored and needed entertainment. That was also why he had cigar and cigarette burns all over his body, and why his hair had been pulled out in clumps. He hurt all the time in his little black prison.

He wasn't in a prison. He was in a metal box, surrounded by his own stinking fecal matter. Once a day, and never at the same time, the enemy would open a small slot at the base of the box by his feet. They would shove a plastic bottle of water through it, as well as something to eat. It was never a meal; if he got a quick glance in the daylight, he could sometimes identify what the food was, but more often than not, he couldn't. They usually gave him a hard, moldy slice of bread or some flat, hard thing that he thought might be a dried-out tortilla. One time, they shoved a chunk of cheese through the slot, and he had been so excited! But when he bit into it, his mouth was filled with fuzzy mold, and he had vomited immediately.

∞

Laughter came; the sounds startled him, it was loud, almost right next to him. Men spoke rapidly in their native tongue, and he could tell they were cracking jokes by the laughter that came in response to the words. Suddenly, something hit the metal box with a loud crash; he jumped and cried out, his entire body shaking as he tried to brace himself for the unknown. They had come to have a bit of entertainment, he knew; it wasn't the first time.

Another crash, then more laughter, louder now. He kept his eyes closed all the time; there was no use for them in the dark, and it seemed he could hear better if he weren't straining to see. Yes, they were all around him; he pulled his knees to his chin and rested on them.

The slot opened, giving him yet another jolt. One eye and part of a nose appeared in the slot, blocking out what little sun was trying to come in. The eyes were smiling; they were having fun like this horrid war was a day at the amusement park.

The man spouted something out in Arabic, then all of his friends in the background roared with laughter. The soldier waited for a response from him, but he remained silent, his eyes clenched, his lips moving at the speed of light as he begged. Angry at being ignored, the soldier repeated his words, but this time his voice had an edge to it, and he didn't wait for an answer. The slot clapped shut, and suddenly the soldiers outside began to strike the box on all sides, over and over, yelling profanities and who knows what else as they did so. They struck the box so hard it dented, hitting his head and body with every blow; he continued to struggle not to cry out.

Suddenly, they stopped hitting the box. He could hear them talking, one on each side of the small confinement, which was barely a four-foot cube. He held his breath, waiting for whatever was to come next. Without warning, the box was violently lifted from the ground and flipped over; his head struck what was now the bottom of the box so hard that he began to see stars, and his hearing faded in and out. The men laughed, but he didn't register the sound.

By the time his head cleared, he could hear them no more. He remained frozen for some time, upside-down, his neck bent to relieve his weight from his head. They had done this before, and he knew it would take a long time to get himself into the upright position. His body hurt so badly that it was a struggle from beginning to end.

CHAPTER 1

Present day

"Ladies and gentlemen, this is your Captain speaking."

Jason Brandtley stirred slightly in his sleep, his light snoring interrupted. He didn't hear the announcement, though it did attempt to break into his dreams. Instead, he simply adjusted himself in his seat and tried to settle back into dreamland.

"We are currently twenty minutes from our scheduled arrival at Cheyenne Regional Airport, and I am pleased to say we will be landing ten minutes ahead of schedule. Please prepare your belongings for landing; we will notify you shortly when it is time to buckle up. We hope you enjoyed your flight, and thank you for flying Northwest Airways."

Jason's eyes fluttered a bit. He opened his eyes into a slit and shifted them from here to there without moving another muscle. He was on a plane, and it was full of civilians. Jason's heart, which had briefly skipped a beat at the Captain's words, began to slow down; he had nothing to worry about... it was okay.

He was on his way home.

Suddenly, the back of his seat was bumped hard, twice, jerking him in surprise and spurring the tremors that plagued him whenever he was taken off-guard. Jason jumped, wide awake now, and spun around to look at the seat behind him. His eyes were wide, and his lips trembling. His right hand reached for his hip while the other groped at his chest, but he wasn't armed. At the same time, he met the eyes of a young blonde woman who was attempting to pry her child off her lap and buckle him into the seat next to hers. She smiled at Jason ruefully.

"Sorry about that," she said, embarrassed. "He's so tired; he got me a couple of times, too."

Jason glanced at the chubby blonde boy struggling in his mother's arms. The kid's face and t-shirt were smeared with chocolate, and he had a runny nose. He was squirming violently and grunting in defiance as his petite mother fought him into his seat.

The boy had kicked the back of his seat, that's all it had been.

Jason turned around and leaned his head back, a long sigh escaping his lips. He had to chuckle after a minute; the war had taken a terrible toll on him, and he was an emotional wreck. He was so glad to be going home.

Taking a moment to get his head on straight, Jason finally opened his eyes and looked for his safety belt. He grabbed the end with the heavy buckle, then leaned forward to pull out the other end, which was wedged into the seat behind him. He tried to give it a good yank, but he couldn't get a good grasp on the heavy nylon belt at all.

"My hand," he muttered in disgust.

Jason gently laid the buckle down on his lap, then used his right hand to free its partner. He was then able to steady the end with the clasp with his lame hand and guide the buckle onto it with his right. Soon, the belt was snug around him, and he gave his hand a sneer.

They had told him he would never have complete use of that hand. The doctors at Fort Lewis had done four surgeries in an effort to get it as close as possible to normal, but it would never be the same. He had limited feeling in the hand, and he could make no more than a sloppy open fist with it. It's sad, but he was thankful in his own way. After his rescue, his hand meant a guaranteed one-way ticket home, and he'd had enough of the War on Terror to last him a lifetime.

He still woke up screaming, and the psychiatrist at Fort Lewis had told him that could last anywhere from a few months to many years. His nightmares about being in the box plagued him to the point that he couldn't take being in a small bathroom, much less wake up in the darkness. It was so bad that for the first two months at the fort, they would find him in the night, curled up in the corner with his knees to his chest, his head down, and his arms covering him for protection as he slept.

It had been a terrible thing to live through, being a prisoner of war. He had heard things and read things his entire life about people who had endured the same type of torture, but he never understood the depth of their agony until it happened to him. The fact was, Jason Brandtley would never be the same again, and he knew that all too well.

A ding sound filled the air. "Please fasten your safety belts…" The soft, feminine, computer-generated voice was followed by the Captain's, who told them all to prepare for landing before thanking them once again. Jason could really do without all of the repetitions. He had his head back once again, and his eyes were squeezed shut in preparation for the landing. There had once been a time that Jason loved to fly; now he found himself struggling at the very thought of touching down.

The pretty brunette flight attendant was making her way up the aisle to check seatbelts. Her smile was made of plastic, and it didn't even come close to touching her eyes. All of the kindness came on-demand, as required. Soldiers are a lot like that, Jason thought as he peered at her through well-practiced slits in his eyelids. She reached him, looked at his belt and that of the old man next to him, and flashed her fake smile. Jason smiled back weakly, then quickly turned away.

The plane began to land, and it wasn't smooth in any way, at least not to him. He held his breath, stopping only to quickly refill his lungs here and there. With eyes tightly closed, he repeated his safe words in his mind the entire time, until finally, after an eternity, the massive plane came to a stop.

Jason breathed as all the passengers began to move about all around him.

Jason sat still, his safe words playing over and over in his mind like a scratched disc. When he had started therapy while hospitalized at Fort Lewis, creating the safe words was one of the first things Dr. Hanson had him do to help battle his condition: Post-Traumatic Stress Disorder with Anxiety. The safe words could be used in any place, at any time, and Jason used them often. Countless times he had been thankful for them, and for having someone in his life to provide him with that tool. Truth be told, if not for those words, Jason would have likely killed himself while still in the hospital.

The words were his own, chosen from his own fond memories of days gone by before he enlisted and went overseas to fight for the country's freedom. Days before he was rudely thrust into the harsh, violent reality of life. His safe words consisted of one short phrase, uttered by his father on countless occasions to him before his untimely death. He heard them as a child when he was hurt, he heard them when his first and only love cruelly dumped him, and he heard them with every bad grade and failure he faced.

'I love you, Son, and there is always tomorrow.'

That was it; his safe words were simple. The sentence consisted of a meager nine words, but it was as powerful to Jason as a paragraph, or maybe even a book. Every time he ran them over and over in his mind, his eyes clenched shut and his world caving in, the safe words covered him like a blanket of warmth and love.

Dr. Hanson had also assigned him to listen to classical music. Jason had grown up around country and western music, but he had always loved the defiance and freedom of rock and roll. When Dr. Hanson gave him the assignment, which had initially been to listen to a handful of selections a day to promote personal stillness and peace, he had groaned aloud. But, true to form, he obeyed. Before long, Jason had the music constantly playing, pumping through an mp3 player he signed out from the nurses' station on his wing. Dr. Hanson had been right; the music worked miracles, calming his nerves, shutting out chaos, and soothing his angry, traumatized soul. Now Jason hardly listened to anything else, and he wished he had thought to keep the small used mp3 player Dr. Hanson had gifted him, but he had packed it safely in his luggage. When he got home to his mother's, he would play some of the beautiful sonatas and requiems that brought him so much stillness.

Finally, people were clearing out, and Jason had enough room and oxygen to stand and retrieve his carry-ons from the overhead compartment. He was the last person to file off the massive jet, smiling with relief as he walked through the jet bridge toward the airport. He had made it through the flight without any incident, now to get his bags and get a cab home.

∞

Within twenty minutes, he was standing on the curb outside the airport's main doors, staring at the long line of taxicabs and other vehicles waiting to pick up those who had flown into Wyoming. People were scrambling, hollering, and even pushing past each other to get to the cars for hire first, taking no one else around them into account. Jason stood patiently waiting for the chaos to die down; he was more than willing to let others go before him, especially if it meant keeping himself mellow and still.

"Jason?"

Hearing his name, he jerked his head to the right, then the left, scanning the crowd for the source.

"Jason! Over here!"

Looking slightly over his shoulder, Jason finally saw a familiar face, and a smile broke out easily and honestly. Dropping his bags, he immediately opened his arms, and an older gentleman with white hair and a green plaid shirt gruffly pulled him into a bear of an embrace.

"Boy! It's good to see you home safe and in top condition!"

Jason hugged the man back, squeezing him harder than he even realized. His eyes were closed, and he smelled the scent of cigars on the plaid shirt; it was the smell of home. He had dreamed of a moment like this for so long.

"Dale!" Jason tried to keep the tears from falling by closing his eyes tightly, but a tear escaped and ran down his cheek anyway. "You don't know how badly I've missed you!" He stepped back and looked at the ranch hand he had known his entire life, his own father's best friend. "I didn't expect you, Dale. I was waiting to get a cab, but as you can see…"

Dale Cassel stood back and put his hands on Jason's shoulders, looking him in the eyes. Dale's own eyes were shining with joy as he looked at the young man standing before him. Jason's smile was both shy and sheepish, and he could feel the blood rising to his cheeks as Dale gazed upon him.

"Let me get a good look at you." He stepped back slightly, keeping his hands on Jason. Now Dale looked him up and down. "Got all your parts, yep. That's a good thing. How are you feeling son?"

As he dropped his hands to his sides, Jason shrugged. "Good, I guess. My hand's a mess; can't really do much. But the rest of me is intact."

Dale nodded and studied him for a moment. "How's the old noggin though, boy?" He tapped twice on his temple with his forefinger, his smile still in place, but his eyes, serious.

Jason met his look and held it for a second; finally, he sighed. "It is what it is, Dale, but there's always tomorrow."

The man threw his head back and gave a loud, hearty laugh. "Yes, there is! Your dad… what an old rascal! But always full of wisdom. He'd be so proud of you now, Jason."

Dale bent down to grab at Jason's bags, which sat forgotten on the ground by his feet. He snatched up one suitcase, but Jason made haste to grab the other, plus his two shoulder-strapped carry-ons.

"I can get that, you know," Jason scolded.

Dale clucked at him. "Don't be silly. Now come on,

let's get moving. Your old mom might be laid up, but she's still sassy as a pistol. If we make her worry, we'll both get strung up. My truck's in the twenty-minute lot." He motioned with a jerk of his head. "Let's get out of this madhouse… what do you say, kid?"

"Let's do it!"

∞

Within fifteen minutes, Dale was turning his big truck out of the airport and onto the main road. It was a beautiful August day, sunny and still, perfect for eleven-thirty in the morning. The rest of the day would be exceptional as well, and Jason could hardly wait to get back to the old ranch and see how it looked. His mother had written to him that things had gone a bit 'downhill,' as she put it, but he knew that she wouldn't have let things go too far.

"How is Mom, anyway?" he asked as Dale took a left onto the interstate.

The old man clucked again. "You know your mom. Signe's a tough cookie, but she won't ever admit it if she isn't feeling up to par. Just between us, she never does anymore. Well, old Doc Harper's got her on so many pills and such, I don't even know how she knows her own name half the time." He chuckled and shook his head, then his smile faded. "The truth is, and she never will tell you this herself, but she isn't doing so hot."

Alarmed, Jason turned abruptly to him. "What do you mean?"

"Now, don't get all worked up. Signe told me she wrote to you about the cancer and told you the truth;

did she?" Dale glanced over at him briefly before looking back at the road.

Jason looked down at his hands and began to fiddle with his fingers. "Yeah. I mean, I guess. She told me she has cancer; wrote to me about it last year. Anyway, she told me what treatments she was getting, and she said if they didn't work for her, she probably had two years left."

Dale glanced at him again. "Well, that's all mostly true. But she doesn't have two years, son. She saw the specialist last week, and his outlook wasn't good."

"Well?"

Dale took a deep breath and pretended to concentrate on traffic, but the road was pleasingly clear. "Jason, she should probably tell you this, but she won't. She thinks you've been through enough, and you have; you've been through a lot. But a man deserves to know when his mama's ailing; he deserves to hear the bottom line." Dale turned to him, his face grim, and made eye contact just long enough to see Jason's face and judge his state of mind. "Doc Harper and the specialist are giving her another two months, but that's a stretch. She's weak, has to stay in bed. Now, don't worry; she has a nurse who stays at the house, so she's well cared for. But, well, it's time for her to be at peace and pain-free, Jason."

He looked out the window and processed what Dale was telling him, and the old man remained silent so he could do so. Jason knew he was right; his mother would never tell him the whole truth. She wouldn't want him to worry or fret after what happened overseas. Signe Brandtley would want him peaceful, happy, able to rest and begin to rebuild his life. The announcement of her impending death would make it harder on him, in her opinion. The truth was if she was that sick and in that much pain, Jason would much rather have her join his father, where he knew she would be happiest.

"We won't tell her you said anything, Dale," he finally replied, offering him a reassuring smile. "We all die; if it makes her life easier to keep me in the dark, then I'm game. But thanks for the heads up."

Dale simply nodded, and from the look on his face, Jason knew Dale was relieved that he wasn't going to have some kind of breakdown. Dr. Hanson had told him that family and other loved ones would try to treat him like he was fragile. Jason knew they didn't know what to expect from him behavior-wise; after all, what is one capable of after being held hostage at war and tortured for nine months before rescue? Worries were likely justified, in many cases, but Dr. Hanson and his time at Fort Lewis had fortified him with tools that would keep him steady and sane.

"On a lighter note," Dale continued, "I have a bit of a surprise announcement."

Jason smiled and raised an eyebrow at him. The tone of the man's voice spoke volumes to Jason; it was playful and teasing. The twinkle in his eye and his use of the word 'announcement' more or less gave it away.

"Don't tell me you've finally found someone worthy of taking the plunge with?" He gave Dale a wink.

Dale Cassel had worked on the Brandtley Ranch for more years than Jason could even remember. Way back before Jason had even been born, his mother and father first bought the ranch in Chesterfield, Wyoming. Dale had been hired on as nothing more than a hand, but it didn't take him long to work his way up to manager. It was at that point when he moved his wife there from Cheyenne, and they took up housekeeping in a small farmhouse about a mile up the road from the ranch. She died about fifteen years earlier when Jason was in junior high; a drunk driver took her out while she was crossing a street in Cheyenne. She had been shopping with Jason's mother for the day, and as the two chatted and laughed while walking, the woman failed to mind the street. She was hit so hard that the car carried her a full block before Signe Brandtley watched the driver brake hard, sending Dorothy Cassel's body flying. He sped away and was never apprehended. Dale's wife was pronounced dead at the scene. Dale always said he would never marry again, that he could never love another, but life has a funny way of calling the shots.

With a smile and a knowing nod, Dale clucked his tongue once again at Jason. "I know, I know. I said I wouldn't do it, but this one took me off guard. Her name is Kay, and she is a retired teacher out of Cheyenne. I met her at Red's Café about six months ago, and she just swept me off my feet. We're going to marry after your mom passes, then we're moving to Florida to enjoy the good life." Dale glanced over at him again. "The ranch needs you, Jason. Things aren't too good; if it's going to live on, well, that's going to be up to you."

"Congratulations… it's about time," he replied. "So, if I know you, you aren't going to give me any details about the state of the place, are you?" Dale shook his head. "Yep, I figured. My mother wants to do it. It's that bad, huh?"

"It's not great."

The two men continued on their drive, chatting loosely about everything from Dale's new love to a new park the town of Chesterfield was building that seemed to be a big debate in the small town. They talked about what Jason's plans were, and how he felt about basically coming home to be alone. He noticed that Dale didn't bring up the war or his personal trauma, and he appreciated him for that.

Before he knew it, Dale was taking a left onto the ranch's long gravel road. As he finished the turn, Jason looked up just in time to see the large sign over the head of the drive reading 'Brandtley Ranch' in large letters. He smiled to himself because now, it was all becoming very real.

Jason Brandtley was finally home.

R.W.K. Clark

CHAPTER 2

She was snoring softly, while the sun made her silver hair glisten, as though there were diamonds hidden within it.

Jason sat in his mother's favorite chair in the corner of her room. He was reclining, with his legs crossed at the ankle out in front of him. As he watched her sleep, he smiled, thinking about the way she used to look when he was a child. Signe Brandtley still looked the same to her only child, yet she was so very different.

He had been a late-in-life baby, born to his parents when they were in their early forties. According to his mother, the doctor had told her and his father, Maverick Brandtley, that they would never have children. They had briefly considered adoption but decided that it wasn't for them in the end. If it were time for them to have children, she would provide them with one. Signe and Maverick had gone on with their lives, working their small ranch and having good times, until one day at a routine appointment with Doc Harper, Signe was told she was with child. According to her, they had never stopped trying and never lost hope.

Now she lay in bed, sleeping soundly, and he

thought of the day she told him this story. Her eyes had been shining brightly, almost glistening with tears. Jason remembered thinking she was the most beautiful mom in the world. He still thought so today.

"Still sleeping, is she?"

Jason turned to see Dale Cassel standing in the doorway. The man was smiling at him; how long had he been standing there? It didn't matter, because he was family.

With a nod, he replied softly, "Yeah, I just don't have the heart to wake her up. Besides, she looks so peaceful, almost like she isn't sick at all. Her hair held up well."

Dale made his way into the room and took a seat on the handmade cedar chest Jason's father had crafted for one of his mother's birthdays. "She opted to pass on the chemo; all of us tried to get her to do it, but you know your mom. She always said when her time was ready to take her, she wasn't going to struggle. The one thing she agreed to was pills for the pain. She's a trooper, your mom."

"I know."

Signe's snoring suddenly was cut short, and her eyes began to flutter. "Rick? Is that you?"

Her husband had been dead for some time, but in her sleepy state reality was eluding her. Jason rose and walked to the bed, kneeling next to it and putting his hand gently on her arm. He waited as she tried to focus her eyes and mind. Signe peered at him through tired, narrowed eyes, then a smile broke out on her face.

"Jason!"

The woman tried to sit up, but it was a far more difficult task than she expected. "Hold on, Mom. Let me get some pillows behind you."

Jason made the needed adjustments, his mother gazing at him with deep love and admiration the entire time. He tried not to make eye contact right away for fear that he would break down; the reality was hitting home now. Signe Brandtley was dying.

"There you go; how's that?" he asked.

"Oh, it's perfect! Now, let me look at you."

Jason sat carefully on the side of her bed and let her take one of his hands into hers. Her eyes scanned his face with joy, but she didn't say anything right away. It was as if she was trying to memorize him, to cement this moment in time permanently into her mind.

"You look wonderful!" she said at last. "How long have you been here?" Signe shifted her eyes to Dale, then said sternly, "Why didn't you wake me? I told you to wake me as soon as you got here with him, Dale Cassel!"

Dale shrugged, crossed his arms over his chest, and said nothing. He knew Signe, and if he tried to make excuses, no matter how legitimate they were, she would give him a tongue lashing he wouldn't soon forget. Jason was pleased that the man was so much a part of the family that he knew just how to handle her.

Signe turned her attention back to Jason, waving a hand in disgust at the old ranch hand. "Phooey on him. I'm so glad you're home."

"So am I," he replied. "Dale tells me things are needing a bit of attention around here. Is it bad?"

Signe grunted a bit and tried to adjust herself, so she was sitting more upright. Jason stood to help, but she waved him off, and soon she was settled back in the way she wanted. He sat back down on the bed just as a woman rapped gently on the open bedroom door.

"Excuse me," she greeted them with a pleasant smile. "Sorry for interrupting; Signe, I just wanted to see how you were feeling. Do you need any of your medication?"

The woman thought about the question for a moment, pausing to see how her own pain was. "I think I'm fine for now, dear. But if you'd make me a bit of soup… beef barley sounds good I think, I would appreciate it." Her eyes lit up, and her hand went to Jason's leg. "Here he is, Michelle! My son Jason, home and all in one piece! Jason, this is Michelle Reed. She's my live-in… for now, anyway. At least until this is finally over."

His mother's words stung his heart, but Jason forced a smile anyway. "Nice to meet you, Michelle. Thanks for all you do; hopefully I'll be of some help around here for you."

"Nice to meet you, too," the full-figured blonde replied. "Glad you're here, I've heard so much about you; your mother is so proud. Signe, I think I'll get that soup warmed."

She ducked out of the room, and Signe cleared her throat. "About that, Jason. Michelle won't be needing any help; I've let her go."

His smile quickly faded. "Why? In your state, you need her here." He glanced at Dale, who simply shrugged. Sometimes he could be infuriating; certainly, the man knew of his mother's plans, yet had neglected to tell him.

"Well, for one, you're here now," she replied as she stroked his thigh. "Jason, the truth is, the doctor doesn't think I'll see the month out. I don't want some third wheel hovering over me. I'm dying, Son. Let me do it my way. You'll have your chance to go out someday, believe me; then you can call the shots."

Jason stared at her in disbelief, then shot another look at Dale, who was pretending to be very interested in something out the window. Jason groaned inwardly. It wasn't that the thought of caring for his mother scared him; he simply wanted her to be in the best hands possible, and he wasn't sure those hands were his.

"Mom, what if something happens? What if you fall?"

Signe chuckled. "Then you call the ambulance, Jason. Stop fretting. I can make it to the bathroom on my own with my walker. The only thing I really need you to do is bring me food and medicine. I'm dying, but I'm not crippled. A little weak, perhaps, but crippled? No."

"Dale?" Jason was trying to find a hole to run through, but the man was having no part of it.

The ranch hand stood. "Don't look at me. I'm going out to get some coffee. You'd better fill Jason in on the technicalities, Signe." With that, he left the room.

Jason turned to her. "Well, what's the bottom line, Mom?"

Signe took a deep breath. "The ranch isn't as booming as it used to be, bottom line. We have over two hundred head of sheep, but just two horses left: Winnie and her last colt, who happens to not be a colt anymore. We call him Rayne. I'm leaving all of it to you; do with it as you please."

He turned his attention to his hands, which were clasped together in his lap. When it came to the bequeathing of the ranch to him, that was no surprise. He was an only child, and his relationship with his parents had been long and satisfying, full of love and completely lacking in bad blood. Yes, him getting the ranch was a given.

"So, I don't care what you do with the sheep," she continued with a sigh. "Dale will give you all the details. I'm sure he told you that he is going to be married. Since you're home, his last day will be Saturday; he never did work on Sundays, as you know. I guess on Monday, he and Kay are going to make their way slowly to Florida; they'll be visiting her sisters along the way." Signe smiled, a distant look in her eyes. "Dale's so excited, you know, like a kid, almost. Rick would have been tickled to see him finding someone to be with."

She focused her eyes on Jason again. "Anyway, enough of that. So, before he leaves, he will spend his last few days giving you all the details. Let's see, I was talking about the sheep before... Oh, yes! We have contracts with a couple of textile mills, one in Jackson and the other about twenty miles outside of Casper. I can't think of their names right now." Her hand went to her temple, and she closed her eyes.

"We don't have to do this right now, mom," Jason uttered sternly. "I'm not going anywhere; I'm home for good."

Signe's eyes shot open, and she dropped her hand quickly. "No, you might not be, but I am. As I was saying, you can continue with the sheep or get rid of them; it makes no difference. As for the horses, Winnie's in bad shape; her hips are shot, Jason. She has her good days and bad, but we do give her shots of tranquilizer and painkillers to help her. I just can't bring myself to put her down. If you can, well, more power to you, but you'll see; she has her good days."

Winnie had been in his life for over twenty years; she was part of the family. At twenty-eight, he could hardly remember a time that she didn't exist. It would be painful having to put her down, but if she were that bad, he would have to follow through.

"Jason," Signe muttered.

He turned quickly and looked at her. "Yes, Mom?"

With a slight smile, his mother said gently, "You can sell the ranch if you want to. Now, I know you would never want to tell me if that was your intention and to be honest, I don't want to know if it is. But if it is, I just want you to know that I wish you would reconsider. This is your home, and whether it's a working ranch or not doesn't matter; it can be anything you want it to be.

Someday you'll take a wife, and you'll have this stability; it will be yours, free and clear."

Jason gave her a smile and took her hand lovingly into both of his own. Looking her directly in the eyes, he said, "I promise you, right now, from my heart, the thought of selling the ranch has never crossed my mind. I appreciate all you and Dad have done to secure my future."

With that, he leaned over and hugged her, noting how bony and fragile she felt, almost as if she would snap in two if he squeezed too hard. She had always been tiny, but now she seemed as small as a child. The realization brought a tear to his eye.

Signe embraced him weakly, then pushed him away. "Now, get out of here and send that girl in here with my soup and a pain pill, will you?"

"I love you, Mom."

Signe glowed at him. "I love you too, Jason Dean. Now, scoot!"

Just as he had always done, Jason obeyed his mother, and just as it always had, it warmed his heart to do so.

∞

"So, Boy," Dale boomed as he clasped Jason's shoulder firmly, "here's the deal with the sheep: Mason's Textiles up in Jackson is one of our contracts, and the other is by Casper, Randolph Textiles and Fabrics. Now, these contracts bring in about forty grand a year, which is nice. One man is working them for your Mom right now; I'll introduce you in the morning.

Name's Kirk Hampton; he's a good man, about forty-two, moved to Chesterfield about a year ago with his wife and ten-year-old daughter. He comes about five in the morning and tends them, then returns after lunch and leaves about five in the evening. He won't bother you none if he doesn't have to unless there's a problem."

The two men had been walking the property, making their way to the fenced field that the sheep called home. Jason could see the gate to the pasture ahead, and in the distance, the grazing sheep. To the right were their shelter and their food and water troughs. When they reached the gate, both men automatically rested their elbows on the top rail and peered across the pasture.

"Anyway, you know it's a good profit, and there is minimal work and cost; they pay for themselves." Dale shifted his gaze to the sky. "So, you think you might keep them?"

Jason didn't even have to think about it; the Army hadn't made him rich. "I need them. Limited income on disability; I need all the help I can get."

"Good." Dale gave him another firm slap on the shoulder. "You know how things work; you'll do fine."

Jason turned to him. "I'm not worried about that; I know I'll do fine. It's just that since... well, since being away, I don't really take to new people very well. I just don't want the guy hanging around right now. Not to be rude."

"I understand." Dale took his hand off Jason and

put his arm back on the rail. "Here's the good news: you're not gonna have to worry about that. He's not really a social type, he's all business. He's friendly, and he does a good job. Been here eleven months and hasn't missed a day. Enough of this; let's go look in on Minnie and Rayne."

The two men turned and began walking the short distance back to the stables. On the way, they continued their chat, catching up a bit on local town gossip that Jason had missed during his absence. He could tell, more than once, that Dale wanted to ask him about the war and what had happened to him. But with each suspicious pause, he would change his mind and bring up some random person or topic, tactfully changing the subject.

"Okay," Dale stated as they approached the small stable. "Like your mother told you, Winnie's hips are pretty much shot, but she has her good days and her bad days. To be honest, up until the last couple of months, there was more good than bad, but recently she's taken a bit of a turn for the worse."

They went through the gate, and as Dale closed it up, Jason looked around. He could see the back of Winnie's head; she was looking out the rear of the stable into the pasture, watching her colt, as he grazed. While he couldn't see her eyes, Jason thought that her demeanor was off. In the past, Winnie would have been right along with Rayne, grazing and wandering around out there. But even from the rear, he could see that she was a bit forlorn, standing there, just staring wistfully.

"She stays in most of the time now?" he asked.

Dale offered a nod as they slowly headed toward her. "You'll see when we get closer that she can go out if she wants; the door is open. But she's just so tired, it seems all she can do is stand there and watch. On her bad days, she doesn't even stand; she'll just lie down and moan. It's heartbreaking."

As they got up to the stable, Winnie turned to them. Upon seeing them, she tried to turn her large body around to face them and get some attention, but she struggled to do so, even wincing a bit now and then.

Dale turned to Jason. "See? Yep, it's not good."

"So, what about the medicine?"

The ranch hand reached out and began to stroke the old mare. "Well, when she gets anxious and begins fussing a lot, we give her a shot to calm her, and it works wonders for her pain. These are given epidurally, by the way; you remember how to do that?"

"Of course, I might have been away, but don't forget, I'm a medic, Dale."

The old man chuckled. "Oh, yeah; forgot about that little bit of information. I'm sure you'll be just fine. The vials and syringes are locked up in the office in the house, and the dosages are printed out and taped inside the lockbox door." He gave her another scratch and gestured toward Rayne, who was heading across the horse pasture in their direction. "You'll know what she needs by her actions. If she's standing and fussing, the pain medicine will do; if she's lying and fussing, choose the tranquilizer. Now, it takes hold in about twenty minutes."

Jason reached out and began to give Winnie some scratches under her chin. He remembered when she was young, energetic, and virile, and he felt sad and sick. This was life; this was what happened to you after you had given your all.

After a moment, Dale asked hesitantly, "Have you thought about putting her down?"

Jason shrugged without looking at him. "I guess I'm gonna give it a bit and see how she acts and how I feel about it. I'm not gonna let her suffer too long. If I have to, I'm not afraid to call Doc Gale and take care of things for her sake."

Dale gave a bittersweet smile. "Good. I knew you'd have your senses about you. Your mother can be so difficult about things like this."

The pair spent another few minutes at the stables, loving on Winnie, and giving Rayne plenty of attention when he reached them. They gabbed loosely about things, and Jason knew that Dale was trying to keep things light, for his sake. This was a lot to absorb, but Jason was just the man for the job. Regardless, it didn't hurt any less to face things; all of it was like a hard slap from the stinging hand of reality. Eventually, life ended; this truth was right in front of him.

Jason Brandtley knew that after what he had been through, he was lucky to be standing there at all.

CHAPTER 3

Signe Brandtley passed peacefully in her sleep two weeks later.

Jason was able to spend a lot of quality time with her during that period, even solidifying his ranch routine during the day. She had progressively gotten worse prior to her passing, even becoming combative and somewhat delusional in her final days; the pain medication didn't help matters. By the time Signe died, it was a relief to everyone who knew and loved her in Chesterfield.

Jason saw to it that she had a beautiful funeral, though he was adamant that it be referred to as a 'celebration of life,' which is precisely what she would have wanted. There were countless people in attendance, including business associates from miles away. He took great satisfaction in the turnout; his parents had been much loved and respected people.

Dale and his fiancée, Kay, had even returned from their road adventure to attend services. The man seemed to be as heartbroken as Jason, though he was also obviously relieved. Signe had been a woman full of life; to see her in the state she was in had been horrible for everyone.

After the services were over, Jason left to carry on the workings of Brandtley Ranch on his own. He took up his parents' mantle like the trooper that he was, facing every day with a positive attitude, which helped to quiet the screaming pain and loneliness constantly surrounding him. Jason was also left with the daunting task of going through Signe's things, which added to his emptiness and heartache. One of the only times he smiled was when he located his beloved Stetson hat, which his father had gotten for him when he graduated high school. Finding the hat had taken the sting away, but only a little.

So, his days became utter routine, but his nights were almost unbearable. During the day, there was plenty to do, between caring for the animals and catching up on other work that had gone neglected around the ranch. The busy work helped to distract him from too much thinking or loneliness. But at night Jason was tortured with his thoughts. Memories of the past ripped at his heart, and flashes from the war tormented his mind. On most nights, he found that he didn't usually even fall asleep until well after two in the morning. There was nothing he could do but continue to put one foot in front of the other.

He wished he had a wife, someone to be by his side as he worked and keep him company during the long hours after the moon rose in the sky. This longing led him to consider his past relationships, which had been few. Where had he gone wrong, and how could he ensure that he never went wrong in those ways again?

Jason thought about how the girls used to treat him in grade school; he had been a bit awkward, even though he was, what the girls considered, 'cute.' They had teased him, giggling and pointing whenever he passed by. His mother had told him time and again that they liked him, that was the reason for their behavior, but that never made any sense to Jason. He simply chalked up his mother's story to her desire to comfort him, and he went on with life.

In junior high, Jason had his first 'girlfriend,' if you could call her that. At that age, kids mostly just hung around together all the time and flirted, still too nervous and scared to really have a 'steady.' Her name had been Darlene Forester, and she had been a chubby girl with brown hair and a pretty face. They had fished together, rode horses at Brandtley Ranch, and rode their bikes in Chesterfield up and down every street in the small town. Darlene had moved away without ever expressing her love or devotion, even though Jason had done so in a long poetic letter, that he gave her on her last day of school. Darlene had never even acknowledged that she had read the letter. Jason never heard from her again, and as time passed, he got over it.

Then came high school, and finally, his first real official relationship. It began in the tenth grade and lasted until the middle of his senior year. The girl's name was Shawna Wieland, and she was born and raised in Chesterfield, just like he had been. The two had known each other as classmates and acquaintances his entire life, though, until tenth grade, the thought of dating had never entered either of their minds.

She had been a bit awkward in junior high, and though Jason had been nice to her, he really hadn't considered her a 'girl,' as strange as that sounded. Shawna had been 'one of the guys,' hanging out with them when they traipsed through the woods, fished, or attended games and parties. Then, on the first day of tenth grade, she walked into his homeroom on air, and Jason hardly recognized her; she had changed something—she was beautiful.

It had taken Jason two months after the start of that school year to work up the nerve to ask her out, but once he did, things seemed to quickly fall into place. They did everything together; where there was Jason, there was Shawna. His parents loved her, and hers, him. It was assumed by everyone in Chesterfield that the two would someday marry and make babies, and Jason assumed it too.

The last month of the summer before senior year, Shawna had gone to her aunt's in Casper for the summer. When she returned, something was off; she was distant, and she seemed to get annoyed easily with Jason, even though he was doing nothing different than he ever had. He couldn't figure it out, and a feeling of dread had filled his heart, nagging him incessantly. Then, right after spring break, Shawna and Jason were out with friends one evening after school. It was then, right in front of all their friends, that she decided to tell him that she had a new boyfriend in Casper, some random guy named Luke she had met during her visit there. She told him they were going to be together forever. She also revealed how nerdy and stupid Jason was, and how she could never be married to some cowboy the rest of her life. She told him Luke was going to be a rock star someday, and he knew how to have a good time. The heartbreak he went through after that breakup lasted him the rest of high school, and it didn't fade completely until he was nearly old enough to legally drink.

He had a couple of dates here and there, but as the old saying goes, once bitten, twice shy. He never really trusted any female completely after that, but now, Jason was at a point where he wanted nothing more than to find the perfect one for him to spend the rest of his life with.

So, he tried to look up Shawna, just on a whim; he even visited her parents one day after getting groceries at the mercantile in Chesterfield. He stopped by just to say hello, but secretly hoping that maybe Shawna was around. If she was, perhaps they could have another chance. After all, their breakup had taken place ten years prior.

According to her parents, Shawna had married Luke, and he had taken her down a terrible path indeed. The last the Wielands knew, their daughter and Luke were living somewhere in Montana; the couple had married, divorced, and even had a couple of offspring. The pair got strung out on drugs somewhere along the line, and his parents took the toddlers while Shawna and Luke gallivanted around. By the time Jason left the Wieland home, he felt like he had dodged a major bullet when it came to Shawna, even though he still felt the heartache of her rejection.

Often, Jason thought about these things because the pain of these truths was far easier to handle. Then the horrifying ache that accompanied memories of the war, memories of the metal box that he had called home. Even though he hurt over the past and the girls he had known, he held onto hope that someone was out there for him, and he wouldn't give up on trying to find her. Even the trauma and the lingering responses which it had induced couldn't keep him from that.

∞

"You know, Jason, whenever you're ready to put her down, I'll fully support you in that."

Dr. Dick Gale, Chesterfield's veterinarian, sat at his desk puffing on a smelly cigar. Jason sat across from him, listening to his words of support. He had come into town for the sole purpose of seeing Doc Gale to get more tranquilizers and pain meds for Winnie, but the errand also gave him a good excuse to visit the old man who had been his father's friend for so many years.

"Your mom talked to me briefly about what you had gone through over there." Doc Gale sat forward and stubbed out his half-smoked cigar, then put his elbows on his desk and leaned toward Jason. "I'm sorry son. Have you talked to anyone since you got home?"

Jason squirmed uncomfortably in his chair and offered Dick a brief smile. "Yeah, yeah. Don't worry about me, I'm fine. I have a lot of little tricks I use to get me through. The past has passed, and I guess I just want to leave it there."

Dick studied him briefly, then offered a nod of resignation. "Okay," he said as he stood. "But remember, I'm always here if you need to talk, son. So, tell me, are you settling in okay up there at the ranch?"

Jason stood, and the two started out of the office. "Actually, I'm doing surprisingly well. It all came back to me fast and easy, like second nature."

They stopped at a small refrigerator in the main work area. Doc Gale opened it and fished out three vials, then took two packages of syringes from a box on a high shelf. He put them in a bag, along with a copy of a prescription which he had in his pocket.

"As you know, Winnie has a running script for these things," he said as he handed Jason the bag. "I'll continue to fill them on demand until she either passes or you're ready to put her down. Remember, Jason: you don't have to keep her around just because Signe was stubborn; you know that, right?"

"I know," he replied, taking the bag. "I guess I just want a little more time with her. To be honest, I don't think I'll put her through much more of it, though. I didn't think I'd need this right away, but I used the last up a couple of days back. When she woke me this morning, crying like she was, I came in. But if she wakes me again like that, well…"

Doc Gale nodded. "All you have to do is call me, and I'll come to take care of it."

Jason remembered that the landline telephone had been disconnected shortly after his mother's death. "I guess I'd better get it turned back on," he contemplated after telling the vet about it.

"Well, don't you have a cell phone?" Doc Gale asked.

Jason shook his head. "Funny, but I hadn't even thought of that. I guess maybe I'll take a trip to Cheyenne tomorrow and get one. Crazy, but I hadn't even considered that I might need one."

Doc Gale walked him out to the old brown truck that his father had gotten for him. Jason opened the driver's side door and put the bag of medication on the seat, then turned back to the vet. He smiled and shook the man's hand.

"I'd better get back and tend to Winnie," he said. "Thanks for the help, Doc."

"No problem, Jason," the man replied. "Remember, if you need more, just give me a ring, day or night. I'll take care of you."

Jason pulled out of the lot with nothing but the horse on his mind. He wiped out any other thoughts and aimed his truck back toward the ranch. Maybe Doc Gale was right; maybe he should just put Winnie down.

But at the last second, for no particular reason, Jason thought he would keep her around a while longer.

CHAPTER 4

The drive home was uneventful, and Jason was able to quickly take care of Winnie's pain and get her comfortable before heading into the house to make something to eat for himself. Kirk Hampton, the hand who tended the sheep, arrived just as he was reaching his front steps; the two men greeted, talked about the weather for a bit, then Jason let him get to his own duties.

Once inside, he made a sandwich with turkey, swiss cheese, and mayo then went into the office and booted up the computer. He needed to enter the new vials of medicine into the inventory, plus put them into the accounting program so he could keep track of the expenditure. Jason figured he should also get a cell phone. Time to catch up to everyone else in civilized society; after all, he had a ranch to take care of and no means of communicating with anyone while he was at home. With Winnie being in such bad shape, Doc Gale was right: he needed to have some kind of phone.

Jason ate his sandwich preoccupied—his mind is far too focused on getting a cell phone. By the time he was finished eating, he had decided to visit the company his own father had used for cellular service: WyCell. He didn't know much about any of it, but he was confident that whoever got him going on the service would be more than happy to explain things to him.

When he was finished with the bookkeeping, Jason went out and gave Winnie a check, noting that Kirk was gone and all seemed well with the sheep. He thought about Kirk; the guy was exactly the kind of help he needed on the ranch. He didn't linger or try to talk too much. Instead, he came on time, did his job, and left without any bother whatsoever. It was a great relief to not have to hold anyone's hand. Truth be told, Jason wished he had someone to hold his hand.

So, he puttered around the place, doing this and that as he saw the need. By five he was starving, needed a shower, and thought that a movie sounded good. Jason kept it simple that Tuesday; he microwaved a TV dinner, got cleaned up, and then planted himself in front of the massive flat-screen that hung on the wall over the fireplace mantle. As he scrolled through the channel menu, he thought of his father, Maverick, and smiled; he always had been good about keeping up with technology. Jason was more like his mother, if he didn't have to bother with it, he certainly wouldn't. Unfortunately, times were changing so fast that he had little choice but to concede.

He chose an old movie that one of the channels offered, and settled in for the evening. He had seen the flick a thousand times; his father had loved old movies. For most of the movie, he was alert and aware, but before it was over, Jason was snoozing peacefully on the couch, an afghan his grandmother had made draped over him. It wasn't until almost two in the morning that he woke with a start; had someone kicked the outside of his box?

Jason sat upright abruptly, confused by his surroundings. The light from the television, then the words coming from it, jerked him from his nightmarish daze. He was home, covered in sweat and shaking, but home. Standing, he grabbed the remote control, shut off the set, then made his way to the bathroom. He needed his medication to help his anxiety and possibly get him back to sleep faster.

Back in the living room, Jason turned on the stereo system. He had a compact disc changer that held two-hundred discs, and the thing was loaded with the finest classical music on the planet. He kept the changer set to shuffle at all times, and there were speakers all over the house so that no matter what room he was in at any given time, he could hear the soothing notes that seemed to comfort him the way his mother once had when he was a child.

The sounds pumped through the speakers as he climbed beneath the thick down comforter that covered his king-sized bed. The bed always seemed so massive at times like this, times when he had his panic attacks and nightmares. Someday, he would share this bed and this big old lonely house with someone who loved him.

Jason Brandtley didn't fall back to sleep until dawn.

Cheyenne was a big city by Wyoming's standards, but to the rest of the world, it wasn't that large at all.

Jason drove, humming to a song that pumped through the speakers and tapping his fingers on the steering wheel. For having so little sleep the previous night, he was in surprisingly high spirits. The sun was shining, the weather was warm, and all seemed right in the world. It was definitely a good day to take a road trip and do a little shopping. The only thing that would have made it better was if he had someone to keep company with on the journey.

He pushed the thoughts of loneliness out of his mind; he had nothing to whine about, nor did he have any excuse for self-pity. Here he was, driving down the highway to Cheyenne for a trivial cell phone, alive and free. Jumpiness and insecurities aside, all the things he longed for would come to him in its time, he was sure of it.

As he entered the outskirts of the city, Jason took the time to soak in as much of it as he could. It was his first trip since his plane had landed weeks ago, and at that point, the main goal was to get home and see his mother. Now, Jason could take the time to stop where he wanted and enjoy the city as he chose. Right at that moment, that meant recognizing places and things and recalling memories of days gone by when he had experienced them. A flash recall about his father while car shopping when he was eight; a mental video of his mother laughing, the wind blowing through her strawberry blonde hair during Independence Day fireworks when he was twelve. He had never said anything to her about how beautiful she was in his eyes, and that truth sent a stab of pain through his core. He put his mind on navigating his way to WyCell, best to worry about the reason for coming to Cheyenne in the first place.

∞

WyCell Cellular was located in a strip mall off Stillwater Avenue. For 9:30, on a Wednesday morning, the place was pretty dead. Classic rock played just loud enough to hear over the speakers; one employee was tending to a customer while the other sat at a desk and scrolled through his smartphone. Jason stood patiently, waiting for someone to take notice of him.

"Mick, you have a customer." The other employee was a brown-haired woman in her thirties. She offered Jason a tight but friendly smile, then went back to her own customer; she took no notice of Jason smiling in return.

"Good morning," Mick said from his left.

Jason jerked his head toward the young man's voice, his shoulders tensing up immediately. Upon realizing that he was being helped, Jason relaxed and broke into a grin.

He closed the gap between himself and the counter and replied. "Yes, sir. I'm gonna need a new cell phone. Oh, and you're likely gonna have to teach me to use it, too."

Mick gave him a pleasant nod. "I think we can get

you up and running today, sir."

∞

Jason whistled cheerfully as he walked to his truck, bag of accessories in one hand, and new smartphone in the other. He didn't have the gadget's workings down pat quite yet, but Mick had given him enough information to wing it the rest of the way. He was a fast-enough learner, so he wasn't too worried about it.

As he pulled out of the strip mall parking lot, the thought of lunch passed through his head. A quick glance at the clock on the dashboard told him it was just before eleven: too early to eat. Jason had toyed with stopping at the tack shop his father had always used to purchase gear for the horses and such. Besides, it would give him a great excuse to visit with the owner, an old friend of his dad's, Hank Ruskin.

'In Tack' had been in business all of Jason's life, and then some. Throughout his twenty-eight years, it had grown and changed, and Hank's wife, Cathy did a great job of keeping up with the times as far as marketing was concerned. Jason found himself getting more and more excited as he neared the place; the couple had always felt a bit like family.

'In Tack' was bustling when he pulled into the lot. Pickup trucks and men with cowboy boots and hats were milling in and out, some with arms laden with just-purchased goods, while others appeared to be casually stopping just to see what was new. Hank and Cathy Ruskin always had a table full of jelly donuts and a piping hot pot of coffee going; it was easy for patrons to decide to hang out for a while.

Jason opened the entrance door to an upbeat country tune and a smiling cashier with a long, sandy braid hanging down her back. As she put a large bottle of what appeared to be horse vitamins in a plastic bag, she offered Jason a flirtatious wink.

"What can we get for you today?" she asked, handing the bag to her customer.

Jason smiled and adjusted his Stetson self-consciously. "Well, I will need something, but for now, I just wanted to know if Hank or Cathy is available."

"Oh!" The girl with the braid turned fully to him. "You know, they took an early lunch today because they had some meeting early this afternoon. I think they'll be back by twelve-thirty." The girl glanced at a large, horseshoe-shaped clock hanging behind her on the wall. "That's more than an hour; maybe you'll want to come back?"

Jason gave the option a brief thought. "You know, I think I might do that some other time. Can you tell me where Hank's keeping the Spirit Animal Horse Rub?"

Kelly smiled and nodded. "Back here, actually. Don't ask me why, but we went through a spot where this stuff was getting shoplifted, along with some other medicinal items. Crazy. Anyway, do you want the small tube or the big tube?"

"Gimme a big one, thanks."

Soon, Kelly was ringing up Jason's, and getting his first name so she could relay a message. He simply told her to let them know that Jason from the Brandtley

Ranch stopped in to say hi. The girl tried to turn on the charm, mentioning that she had a cousin who knew a girl who had lived in Chesterfield once long ago, but Jason just wasn't feeling her vibe. She was cute enough, he supposed, but she was just a bit too bouncy and girly for his personal taste. Maintaining his gentlemanly stance, Jason simply chatted politely, then excused himself, telling her to enjoy her day.

Bag in hand, he climbed back into his truck and got it started, then sat there for a moment, staring at the sack and thinking about his next move. He hadn't wanted to have lunch quite so early, but now it was looking like the best option. After all, he had planned to be back to the ranch by early afternoon, and it wouldn't do to head home now with an empty stomach and all, especially when he was in the city, surrounded by restaurants.

Jason looked around the area, then noticed a deli across the street from 'In Tack.' It was called Randolph's, and the sign boasted the best sandwiches on homemade buns in the history of the world. The claim made him smile; what did the best deli sandwich in 'all the world' taste like? Well, today was the perfect day to find out. His favorite, turkey and swiss with mayo on a lightly toasted bun, seemed to be calling his name from clear over there.

He pulled out of the lot and drove directly across the busy avenue and into the Randolph's Deli parking lot. As he walked inside, Jason noticed that there was a park across the street to the left of the restaurant;

suddenly, he had the urge to eat his lunch in the sun. Jason smiled and walked into the air-conditioned deli, his stomach offering a growl. Maybe it wasn't too early for lunch after all.

Ten minutes later, he was pulling his truck into a parking space at Gooseneck Park. It seemed he might have visited the park when he was small; a sense of familiarity hit, but he couldn't pinpoint the memory. Pushing it out of his mind, Jason grabbed his lunch, and the cold soda that he had ordered with it, and jumped out, locking the vehicle behind him.

With a quick look around, he saw there were benches near the pond in the middle of the park. People were walking about, and in a nearby field, a group of kids played Frisbee. There was also a hiking trail which began out there in the open, but it disappeared into a long row of trees; people entered and exited the trees, jogging or walking and chatting with a companion. Yes, this was the perfect spot to enjoy a midday meal.

Jason chose a bench at random with his eyes and began to make his way over to it. He plopped down and paused to look around and get a good breath of fresh air. A breeze blew through his hair, and he smiled at the peace he felt; the only thing missing was a nice sonata. It was at times like this that Jason almost believed that the war, and all that happened to him there, would someday be nothing more than a bad dream.

He unpacked his sandwich, opened the bag of chips he had chosen as a side dish, and began to eat. The sound of laughter coming from the Frisbee players caught his attention more than once, but mostly he just watched everything, from the ducks in the water to those walking or jogging. He found himself wishing he did something like this more often; maybe he would even pack a lunch a couple times a week and eat it at Chesterfield Park, just for the sake of getting out.

The sound of a dog yapping filled the air. Jason jumped at the sound and spun his head in its direction. There, at his feet, was a small dog that he guessed was likely a Yorkie. It looked up at him with its round black eyes, trying to ask him for a bite of his sandwich.

A smile came over his face, then he noticed the pink leash dangling from the dog's collar, and the smile faded.

"Are you lost, girly?" He asked the dog in his best doggie voice. "Where's your mama or daddy?" He reached down to pet the animal, his eyes scanning the park; that's when he saw her.

She was running toward him and the dog, saying the dog's name over and over in a somewhat scolding tone. The girl had strawberry blonde hair, the same color his mother's hair had been when he was younger. She was a young woman, no more than five-foot-two or three, and slender, and she was wearing what appeared to be a waitress uniform with a white apron attached.

"Millie!" Now the young lady was much closer; Jason thought she was about his age, maybe a year or two younger. "How many times have I told you not to run from Mommy!"

The girl reached Jason and the dog and snatched up

the looped end of the pink leash. "I'm sorry; she probably smelled your sandwich from a mile away. I swear, it's like her superpower or something!"

She laughed nervously, so Jason gave her a smile to let her know all was okay. "No! She's no problem. As a matter of fact, she's pretty darn cute." He glanced at the dog, then back at the girl, the smile still on his face. "I'm Jason… Jason Brandtley. Just stopped for some lunch in the park before I go back home; I'm from Chesterfield."

The cute girl with the strawberry blonde hair offered a small smile, obviously unsure of him. That was good, he thought; you can't trust anyone anymore. He watched her, without pushing or prodding, but he sure hoped she decided to sit down and chat for a minute. She gave a good look around, taking note of all the other people around them, then her smile grew.

"I'm Andrea Harder," she finally said, her cheeks turning a bit pink. "Sorry about Millie; like I said, she's a bit eager when it comes to the smell of a snack."

Jason chuckled. "No problem; she's adorable. So, did you just get off work or something?" He slid down to the end of the bench, dragging his lunch across with him to make room for her to sit if she chose.

Timidly, Andrea glanced at the empty space on the bench, looked around the park again, then slowly sat on the very edge. Jason turned his attention to his sandwich, taking a bite and gazing out at the pond. He didn't want to make the girl nervous; after all, he wasn't going to hurt her, he just wanted to chat.

"Yes," she finally replied. "As a matter of fact, I did just get off work. I always stop and pick up Millie before I settle in for myself. So, you're from Chesterfield, huh?"

Jason swallowed his bite and nodded. "Yep, born and raised. My family has a sheep ranch there. Well, I guess I should say that I have a sheep ranch; my mother passed not too long ago, and my father's been gone. You from here?"

Andrea shook her head, looking almost embarrassed. "No, I'm kind of a hick; I'm from North Dakota. I've been here for a couple of years, though."

Jason chuckled. "Well, let me tell you, everyone from here is a 'hick'; you have nothing to be embarrassed about. Care if I give her a chip?"

"Sure," Andrea replied, and he tossed a chip on the ground; Millie devoured it, then licked the tiny crumbs from the concrete that surrounded the bench.

"Anyway, I was in the Army," he said casually. "I was a medic overseas, in the war. Just got home not too long ago; still trying to settle in."

Andrea raised her eyebrows. "That must have been hard on your wife and kids."

Jason shook his head. "Nah, no wife or kids. Just my mother was left when I returned. I'm sure it was hard on her for me to be gone, though. You know how mothers can worry."

The girl shrugged. "Well, my mom wasn't much of a worrier, to be honest. Sometimes I would have thought she couldn't have cared less what I did."

Jason studied her. "I'm sure she cared."

"Maybe."

The two sat in silence for a moment. "So, you work close by?" he asked.

She nodded, her eyes glued to a couple of ducks splashing in the pond. "Yeah, two blocks down, at the Cozy Cowboy, best steaks in Cheyenne. I usually work evenings, but this week, I've been filling in days as well for another waitress. Wears me out!"

The Cozy Cowboy, he thought, making a note of the name for future reference. "Are you married? Kids?"

With a shake of the head, she replied, "It's just me and Millie, Millie and me."

Jason glanced up with a smile, but immediately it faded. Andrea was staring at something across the street from the park, her face full of tension and her eyes filled with dread. What was wrong with her all of a sudden?

"Are you okay?" he asked.

She jumped up from the bench and took a couple of steps away from him, tugging Millie's leash as she went. "Yeah, I'm fine. I'd better get going, though. Nice to meet you, Jack."

"Jason," he corrected, but she was already ten feet away from him by that time.

He watched her with concern as she crossed the park, rounded the drive, and disappeared from sight. Andrea Harder, a waitress at the Cozy Cowboy. Jason thought that, whatever was going on to make her rush off, he would like a chance to make it right. She was cute, independent, and had an adorable dog. He sure would like to get to know Andrea better.

He shoved the last bite of his turkey and swiss into his mouth and thought, I'll just give her a little time.

CHAPTER 5

Andrea Harder tried to hustle as she put distance between her and the man in the park. There had been nothing wrong with him; he was nice enough, and he didn't make her uncomfortable. It was just that she had seen Brad's van turning right at the stop sign by the park, which told her that he was cruising by her apartment. Wouldn't he ever get the hint?

Andrea had been dating the abusive Brad Nagle off and on for the past year. He was possessive and temperamental, and more often than not she had left their dates feeling overwhelmed and emotional. He wanted complete control of her life, but she was never one to let anyone control her; her parents could vouch for that.

When she had finally had enough of his abusiveness, she had tried to break it off with him. Several times, Brad acted as though he might finally let things be, but she often caught him cruising around her building, watching her. Once, she even saw him parked out front at four in the morning, and her neighbor told her he had been out there all night. When Andrea confronted Brad, he had told her clearly that she would never be rid of him and in time she would be his, completely. He scared her, but she was determined to eliminate him from her life.

Andrea rushed away from that nice guy in the park a little quickly, she knew, but when she saw Brad's van, she lost her cool. She had glanced over her shoulder at the guy as she fled, twice; he had been staring, watching her disappear for no good reason at all. She hadn't even said goodbye, but oh well.

Stopping across the street from her apartment building, Andrea got a good look at her surroundings. The main avenue was off to the left, about a block-and-a-half up; cars raced back and forth, obliviously going about their business. The park behind her was peaceful and calm, with parents and their children, and the occasional pooch here and there. Her apartment building, as well as the street in front of it, showed no signs of drama or chaos, and Brad's van was nowhere to be seen. Satisfied, Andrea exhaled in relief, then crossed the street to her building.

She was unlocking the main security entrance of the building, thinking how grateful she was for choosing a place that offered that feature, when she heard her name being called sharply from behind her.

"Andrea!"

Without turning, she closed her eyes and groaned. Couldn't she have even a single day without him showing up or calling? Millie began to growl deep in her throat, catching Andrea's attention.

"It's okay, girl," she said soothingly. "It'll be fine."

Turning her attention to the van at the curb, facing the wrong way, Andrea asked wearily, "What do you want, Brad?"

The man shut off his ignition and flashed her a smile full of exaggerated charm. He popped open the door and hopped out, slamming it behind him. There, he stood his place, burying his hands in the back pockets of his jeans and leaning his shoulder against his vehicle.

"I've wanted to talk to you all day," he replied casually. "I left a message at the Cozy; didn't you get it? I would have thought you would have called me back by now."

Andrea did a mental eye-roll and swept the creepy feeling Brad gave her underneath the rug in her mind. "Brad, we've been through this."

"I know, I know. Look, I just thought maybe we could have a beer together, my treat." He stood up straight and removed his hands from his pockets, then crossed his arms over his chest; Brad was beginning to tense up now, she thought. Best to tread lightly from here on out, but caving in is not an option.

She shook her head gently. "No, Brad, but thanks anyway. It won't help the breakup if we keep hanging out. It just creates false hope."

"False hope?" Brad took two steps toward her, causing her to flinch. "False hope? There is no false hope going on here. Do you know why? Well, do you?"

Andrea's entire body was stiff with anxiety. She shook her head while Millie gave a couple of her fiercest yaps. She hated this; at least, she was pretty sure he wouldn't swing on her in broad daylight.

"Because it is what it is," he finished. "We are together, and we will be together in the end; it's just a matter of time until you come around."

He took two more long strides in her direction when suddenly the security door swung open. Mr. Gravitz, Andrea's next door neighbor on her floor, stood there, his chubby hands clenching a shotgun, which he had pointed at Brad Nagle. The old man was sneering, and for someone standing all of five-foot-five, he was very intimidating indeed.

"Seems to me you have a hearing problem, boy," Mr. Gravitz said. "I've distinctly heard this girl tell you countless times that she is through with you. Now, I hate to take these measures, but you need to know I've just about had it!"

Andrea turned to look at Brad, who was standing frozen on the sidewalk, with his hands raised high into the air. "Look, mister, I just wanted to hang out, have a beer; you know, like friends."

Mr. Gravitz just stared at him, sneering, and gave the gun a jerk, signifying that Brad should hit the road.

"You're gonna regret this, Andrea," Brad said as he backed away from the building. "You're gonna wish you made different decisions."

Mr. Gravitz gave the gun another, more pronounced, jerk up the road. Brad stopped at the door of his van, his hands still in the air, and stared at Mr. Gravitz as though he were trying to shake him. But Gravitz got the best of him in less than fifteen seconds, and Brad jumped in his truck, started the engine, and squealed away from the curb, heading for the avenue.

With tears of gratitude and relief welling up in her eyes, Andrea turned to her old neighbor. Chubby Mr. Gravitz, in his plaid golf shorts and all. The man smiled soothingly and held up his hand before she could say anything.

"He's an annoyance," he stated gently. "He's not for you, and you've done right to be rid of him. I'm here to help you through his stupidity. This'll pass, Andrea."

She broke into laughter and gave the old man a great big hug. She may be a grown woman at twenty-five, but sometimes, you just needed someone to have your back. Most of the time, she had to be the tough one, and it drove her crazy when she was alone in the dark.

At least for now, she didn't have to deal with Brad anymore.

∞

Jason Brandtley stood behind the lilac bushes which lined the outer perimeter of Gooseneck Park. He had watched the entire exchange between Andrea Harder, an old man behind her, and some dirtbag in the street. It was obvious to him that Andrea didn't want anything to do with the moron in the van.

So, why hadn't he jumped out of the bushes like Superman? It would have been the perfect way to break the ice. Now he was kicking himself, but at the time, he had considered it for a fraction of a second. That was when he froze solid; the mere thought of confronting the tall, muscular dirtbag had him trembling in his boots.

Andrea and the old man went inside the building, disappearing from view. Jason stood there for several minutes, considering the situation. If the guy had been a boyfriend, he obviously wasn't any longer. Well, regardless, should he even be thinking about trying to run into Andrea Harder again? He couldn't even put one foot in front of the other to protect her.

He stepped away from the bushes, cutting through the grass. As he rounded the slight bend, his truck came into view, but he barely took notice. He was too busy chastising himself mentally to think about anything else. Should he dare hope that he gets a second chance to confront that bum? Probably not, but he was going to give it a go.

Jason jumped into his truck, tossing the plastic bag of garbage from his lunch onto the passenger-side floorboard. As he got on his way back to Chesterfield, his mind swirled around Andrea Harder and Millie, as well as the dirtball who seemed to like to intimidate and frighten her.

He planned to do a little bit of research when he got home. If he intended to sweep Andrea off her feet, he needed to learn a bit more about her, if he could. That was what the Internet was good for, wasn't it? Giving you the information you want, when you want it.

∞

"Thanks, Mr. Gravitz; I appreciate your help so much."

Andrea closed the door to her apartment, locked all

three locks, and leaned back against it with a long sigh. She had just spent the last few hours at the Gravitzes' apartment, eating an early dinner and playing Parcheesi. She would have left sooner, but their hearts were in the right place, thinking of her safety. Plus, they were a lonely old couple, she knew, and they probably enjoyed having her company more than she realized.

Because their living room window overlooked the street, they thought it was best for her to hang out with them for a while and keep watch, just to see whether or not Brad would return. He had driven by the place two more times, but he never stopped or did anything more than stare at the building as he went by. After those two occurrences, the drive-bys stopped, and Andrea knew that he had been sidetracked by a beer at the Watering Hole bar.

Now it was nearly six; she actually had the evening off. First, she was going to take Millie outside for a break in the back. That way, if Brad did drive by again, he wouldn't see her. After that, she planned to soak in a hot bath with candles and wine; she needed to relax.

Millie ended up doing her business fairly quickly, giving Andrea no time to over think things. It wasn't until she was submerged in the hot, soapy water with a wine glass firmly in hand that she let her mind think about the day's events.

Brad, what was she going to do about him? She had really liked him in the beginning, even venturing to say that she had been on the verge of falling in love with him. He wasn't the brightest or best looking, but he had been funny, and he really seemed to be taken with her.

But then he hit her. Andrea had been through this with men before; Brad was just one in a long line. She was at the point, at 25 years old, that if a man hit her once, that was all it was going to take. So, she had tried to break it off with him, but his affection turned into obsession almost immediately. Now, for the last three months, she had been trying to shake him for good, but this bad penny continued to turn up.

If it came down to it, she was more than willing to take legal action, but she always hated to go to that extreme. Why did these dirtballs always have to push things so far? Why did they always have to resort to using their fists?

The first one had been Wade Morgan. Wade had been her boyfriend all through junior and senior high school back home in Shrugton, North Dakota. Andrea had to admit it, the entire town had her convinced that she and Wade would marry after high school, and she would move onto his family farm and raise babies the rest of her life. But when she got the urge to go on a summer adventure to the West Coast with her best friend after graduation, Wade had resisted the idea.

On the night before she was to leave, he called her to apologize for being so selfish about the trip. He wanted her to come to the farm, and the two of them would light a bonfire, and just spend time together before she left the following day.

Andrea went, and it was the first of many bad judgment calls she would make when it came to men.

When she got there, all had been good. They drank and laughed, having an overall good time. But then, as the beers began to flow more freely, Wade announced that she would not be going to the West Coast with her best friend or anyone else. Andrea watched him jumping around, and she listened to his ranting. Finally, she could take no more and tried to leave. Wade Morgan ended up beating her within an inch of her life.

Then, on her twentieth birthday, she met Michael Dunne. Andrea had attended a rock concert with a group of pals from the community college she had been attending. Michael ended up being in the group on the sly; he wasn't a student, just a hanger-on. But he was shockingly good-looking, with a quick wit and personal style to match. She fell head over heels, and in no time, they were moving into an apartment together.

It had been the move that sparked the violence this time around. As soon as he got her into a place that made her 'his,' Michael began to snap on her easily, call her degrading names, and even belittle her in front of his friends. Shortly after that, he began to slap her on the head here and there, lightly at first, but the slaps gradually became harder and more demanding. If she cried out, he often smiled when she did.

Finally, it all came to a head one night when she was late getting home from work. He beat her to a pulp, and he had her so scared for her life that she didn't even attempt to scream for help or call the police. Andrea ended up calling in sick to work for a week, claiming a terrible bout of strep throat. Michael managed to keep his hands off of her long enough for her to heal, making sure she understood that bills were coming due and he needed her to be at work.

There were two other times she had tucked tail and run from him. But he would simply find her, sweet talk her into coming home, then beat her once she walked through the threshold. When her own mother told her she was making up the allegations, Andrea had enough. She began socking money away, and then one day, she hopped on a Roadways bus and high-tailed it out of North Dakota. She got away from him when she came here; moving to Wyoming was the length she had to go to save her own life.

Michael never even showed up on her doorstep since. She found out later from her mother that he had met a wonderful girl who understood him and knew how to treat him right.

Andrea stopped writing or calling her mother after that.

Why had she even let herself get involved with Brad Nagle? She had been free, really free, for the first time in her life when she moved here. No one helped her get on her feet; Andrea had done it all by herself. Maybe she got cocky, thinking she should give love another try since she was independent. It didn't matter; whatever the reason, she had caved in and agreed to date the man who was turning out to be yet another thorn in her side. As far as he was concerned, it was time to get hateful, and not just with him, with all of them. It was time for her to use her own power and let them all know just where they could get off. She was exhausted, and she'd had enough.

The bath water was cooling fast now. Andrea sat forward and pulled the plug, then gently placed her empty wine glass next to the bottle on the closed toilet seat. As she stepped out of the tub and put on her robe, the man in the park flashed into her mind. If my life could only be perfect, she thought.

Jack? Had that been his name? Yes, she thought it was Jack. He seemed nice enough; he had none of that icky vibe that she had always gotten from her boyfriends in the beginning but ignored. He seemed like a simple, everyday sort of dude, the kind who was established. Yes, he was very handsome and polite, unlike all the others; her mind began to race. It didn't matter because he would be just like all the rest. They were all smooth talkers until they got your trust, then it all went down the toilet.

"Best wishes, Jack," she mumbled as she wrapped her hair in a towel. "Hope you find what you're looking for, but that's got nothing to do with me."

That was the last thought Andrea Harder had about the man in the cowboy hat who had shared his potato chips with Millie.

∞

Jason sat at the desk in his father's former office. The computer screen cast a bluish glow on his face and chest as he scribbled furiously in a notebook next to it. Jason had been learning all he could about the girl in the park ever since he returned home. It was now nearly ten at night, and he hadn't even eaten supper.

At first, the search for information had been difficult. He found countless girls named Andrea Harder on the Internet, but from what he could see by the images provided, none of them were her. Finally, after hours of exasperating fruitlessness, Jason was able to track down a little bit. He found a high school yearbook with her photo from Shrugton High, her alma mater, and even located a social media page in her name. He wasn't familiar with social media, but from what he could tell, she had been posting on her page today. Jason wound up creating a page of his own, but held off on requesting her friendship; he was still feeling a bit shy.

So, he continued to find what he could, searching until he felt he would pass out at the computer. He hadn't learned too much, only that she had told the truth when she said where she was from and how long she had been in Wyoming. All the rest he got from social media: she loved Yorkies and the color purple, and she posted a lot of things about being a strong, independent woman who didn't want to be controlled. It made his heart ache to think that someone had victimized her enough to shy away from men like she obviously did.

Jason decided on a light supper of tuna salad on whole wheat with crackers. He topped it off with a cold glass of water and took his food into the living room, where he immediately put on Mozart. Taking a large bite of his sandwich, Jason began to sway, eyes closed, to the beautiful notes of the requiem which seeped alluringly from the speakers.

As he chewed, he wondered if Andrea Harder liked classical music, and he smiled as he made it a priority to find out.

CHAPTER 6

"Doesn't that guy make you nervous?"

Andrea was standing at the point-of-sale terminal at Cozy Cowboy entering a customer's order. She turned slightly to see one of her co-workers standing next to her, her brow knit with disgust. Andrea smiled a little at her and continued to put in her order.

"Who are you talking about, Renee?"

The dark-haired waitress turned around nonchalantly and leaned back against the wall next to the POS station. "The guy whose order you just took. I saw him brush your rear with his hand."

Andrea completed the order and tapped hard on the 'enter' button before turning her full attention to Renee Clovis. The girl seemed to have much more eye makeup on than usual, and Andrea couldn't figure out why Dana, the manager, didn't say anything to her. She looked like she belonged in a brothel, but whatever brought the tips.

"Yeah, he's pretty vulgar," she admitted. "But I can handle him. Let him grab me in the wrong place on my body, at the wrong time of day, and he'll likely lose his head."

Renee snorted. "Do you know how many of us girls would just love to see that?"

Andrea walked to the soda machine and filled up a drink on ice for the guy. "Just so you know, I felt him brush up against me. I've been dealing with Brad a lot lately, so I'm just waiting for this douche bag to give me an excuse." She spun around, soda in hand, and shot a wink at Renee before heading back to the leering man; he hadn't taken his eyes off her.

"Okay, sir," Andrea greeted with a smile as she brought the soda. "Your order is in; it shouldn't be too long."

She started to turn to go, but the man grabbed her by the arm, and none too gently, either. "So, you working late tonight?"

Andrea turned to him once again, smile firmly in place. "I work every second of every day." She tried to walk away for a second time, but the man kept a firm hold on her arm. "Excuse me?"

"There's no reason to be so rude," he told her with a disgusted look on his face. "A pretty young woman like you should have manners, dontcha think?"

She looked down at his hand; he was squeezing her arm so tight that she could see his knuckles turning white. But his grip was giving her no pain. To Andrea, there was no pain right at that moment, only anger at his boldness.

"Fine," she hissed through clenched teeth. "Would you please let go of my arm so I can get back to work?"

His grip loosened, but he didn't set her loose. "So,

back to my question, are you working late? Maybe you and I could get a drink or something." His thumb began to stroke her arm through the sleeve of her uniform, and it made her stomach turn.

Andrea leaned close to him, sneering as she did so. "First, I wouldn't have a drink with you if I was dying of thirst. Second, your lizard hands are rough on my skin; I wouldn't be surprised if no woman lets you touch her."

The customer stared at her, open-mouthed, as he tried to figure out if he had heard her correctly. After a few seconds, he said, "Why, you little…"

"What's the problem here, Andrea?"

'Big Dana' Grulkey, the manager and part-owner of the Cozy Cowboy, had sidled up next to Andrea. Dana stood there with a knowing and a disgusted grin on her face. "I would ask if something was wrong with your meal, except that I happen to know you haven't had it yet. So, are you hassling my server?"

The man's hand dropped into his lap as he picked up his soda with the other and brought the straw to his lips. "You know better than that, Dana. I was just trying to be friendly."

Dana snorted. "Why don't you try being friendly at home, say… to your wife and kids? Might find you've saved yourself a world of hurt and alimony if you were nice to them, wouldn't you think?"

The man grunted and turned his attention to the dessert menu sitting in front of him. Dana gestured with her head for Andrea to take a hike, but she followed. At least Andrea didn't have to worry about being in any trouble for being rude; this guy obviously wasn't a first time offender.

"I don't remember that guy," she muttered as she walked off with Dana. "You know him?"

Dana rolled her eyes. "Yeah, he used to come in here just about every day a few years back, but then he took an over-the-road trucking job. He ain't in here so much anymore, so you don't have to worry. You have enough to worry about with that idiot Brad; he called four times after you left yesterday."

Her shoulders slumped. "I know. I had him giving me flack outside my apartment; my neighbor pulled a shotgun on him! He knew I wasn't here… I'm sorry, Dana."

The woman put her arm around Andrea's shoulders and gave her a squeeze. "Don't worry; I've been in the boat you're in right now. These jerks, the ones that are dirtballs, just don't get it. Nothing he can do will cost you your job. So put it out of your mind."

Dana gave her a pat on the shoulder and headed through the swinging doors that led back to the kitchen and, ultimately, her office. Andrea glanced back over her shoulder to see the jerk customer sneering in her direction; she flashed a snotty smile at him and grabbed a pot of hot coffee so she could make her rounds.

Men… they made her more and more sick to her stomach with each passing day.

∞

Jason stood at the kitchen sink scrubbing his hands, steam from the hot water rising around him as he cleaned under his nails with the brush that had been at the kitchen sink as long as he'd been alive. The hot water distracted him from the pain of the reality he was facing: Winnie the horse had to be put down.

He was just having his lunch, daydreaming about the beautiful Andrea, when he heard the cries coming from the stable, accompanied by loud whinnying from Rayne. Something was wrong, and both of those horses were going to make sure he knew about it. He had jumped up from the table, leaving his meal behind, and ran out in his socks to check on the pained old mare.

He found her lying on her side, grunting and crying out in agony. Jason immediately administered pain medication, making sure to try them in the proper order. But as he worked his way up the line of medications by giving her relief with an epidural, he knew the end was coming quickly. If she started up again, she would be at the end of the line. It would be then that he would have to buck up and call Doc Gale and set up a time for him to come out and put her down.

Jason administered a few shots to help Winnie relax; he waited until the pain medicine took hold. She calmed right down, especially when Jason sat next to her and stroked her. He spoke calmly, soothing words to the mare and within fifteen minutes, she relaxed. Well, he would get through another day, but he didn't have too many of those left with his old horse.

His father's birthday was coming, he thought as he comforted the horse. He knew that if Maverick

Brandtley were still alive, Winnie would have gone to horsey heaven a long time ago. His father had been tough about things like that, even though they hurt him. Well, it hurt him too, and the pain made it difficult to do the right thing. Jason decided right then that he would put the horse down on his dad's birthday, as a sort of gift.

So, he had returned to the house and made the call to Doc Gale. The man would come to the ranch at seven-thirty in the evening on the day his father would have celebrated seventy-eight years of life on Earth. Well, happy birthday, Dad.

As Jason's mind went back to Andrea, he smiled, surprised at how easily she seemed to reside in his thoughts. It was meant to be, he just knew it.

Now it was as simple as working up the courage to approach her again, and making sure the timing was right. He didn't want to just pop up somewhere when that big ox was around, and he certainly didn't want her to think he was some kind of dangerous madman. No, he wanted it to be perfect. He would take her flowers and woo her properly. Jason would show her that his intentions were pure and honest, just the way his father taught him to.

∞

It was time to head to Chesterfield and pick up some more pain medication for Winnie. Doc Gale had told him he would give him enough to last for the next few weeks, which was the amount of time left until his father's birthday, the amount of time left until Winnie would be going to that great big, beautiful pasture in the sky.

When he got back, Jason would see if Andrea happened to post anything on her social media page. He was following her so her posts would be easy enough to spot. If things continued to look like they did for her, and if she didn't change her relationship status, he thought that Saturday night would be the perfect night to surprise her with flowers. He would stop by the Cozy Cowboy and see if she was there first; if she were, it would make the entire nerve-racking process much easier.

R.W.K. Clark

CHAPTER 7

"The tenderloin order was supposed to come with a side of Cozy Sauce! You wanna get that for me?"

Andrea had been at work for a half-hour, and already she was wondering why she bothered. It always seemed to her that, out of the kitchen staff and servers, she was the only one who ever paid any kind of attention to detail at all. The head cook was always messing up, mostly just because he didn't have tips to risk like the servers did. It was infuriating to her, to say the least.

She was scheduled to work nearly twelve hours, from eleven in the morning until ten that night, but it was Saturday; she wouldn't get out of there until nearly eleven. Andrea knew how important it was to not let her exhaustion and disgust show on her face. She had to be pleasant and chipper if she wanted to make that money, but she was so tired. Brad had kept her up until nearly two in the morning, calling and calling, crying and begging, making promises that he never even intended to keep. By two-thirty, she had enough and turned her cell phone off. That hasn't stopped him; he had shown up drunk at her apartment, ringing her at the security door until she was forced to call the police. The cops called a cab for him and made him leave his van. Unfortunately, that meant she had to deal with him almost as soon as she woke up, without even getting a full cup of coffee in her.

This was exactly the kind of drama she had been living with her entire life, even counting her biological and step-fathers: men who didn't comprehend that there was any sort of life existing outside of themselves. Here she was, up late, tired from work, and having to work the next morning again. Yet the guy she had broken it off with was calling her incessantly and ringing her door first thing in the morning. Andrea felt as though she couldn't bear the thought of any more relationships with men. Was there even one out there who cared about anything other than themselves?

The cook slid a small paper container filled with Cozy Sauce across the stainless-steel surface of the food window. Andrea flashed him a quick smile of thanks, snatched up the sauce, and rushed to the table that needed it. As she went, she noticed another waitress seating a new customer at an empty booth in her section. This day was already proving that its sole purpose was to put her in the grave.

"Here you go, ma'am," she said as she put the sauce on the table. "Sorry for the wait."

The woman thanked her, and she started to turn toward the new customer, only to be stopped by another customer grabbing her arm as she passed. He was a regular, a local truck driver who delivered car parts during the week. He flirted with her often, though he had never offended her or made her feel overwhelmed with his presence. Today, he just happened to grab her at the wrong time.

"Hey, Toots!" he greeted. "Looks like you might drown in people today!"

His touch threw her off. Andrea glanced quickly at his face, then glared down at his hand on her arm. "How about you just make sure you aren't one of them. Don't touch; I'm not in the mood!"

The man jerked his hand back as though she had bitten him. "Sorry, jeesh, who got your goat today?"

"Please keep your hands to yourself."

She quickly moved away from his table, stopped at the beverage station, and filled a glass with ice water. Andrea approached the new customer, who was looking over a menu; he looked a tad familiar, but she couldn't place him. Well, all she could do was hope he only wanted to eat and then get out of there.

"I'm Andrea, and I'll be your server today." She sat the glass of water down with a plastic smile on her face, then whipped out her order pad. "Would you like to hear the lunch specials?"

The man immediately looked up at her, his face beaming and his eyes twinkling. "Hi! Um, specials?"

She stared at him, her smile fading. "Yes. The lunch specials; you know, the deals we have for lunch today."

He sat back, still smiling up at her. "I think I know what I want," he replied.

Andrea noticed his brown eyes more than anything

else; it almost seemed as though she couldn't pull her gaze away from them. They were large, and he had long, thick lashes that threatened to tangle together when he blinked. He was a cutie, but she didn't have time for gawking.

"Great," she answered, poising her pen. "What would you like?"

All of a sudden, the stranger pulled a hidden bouquet of wildflowers from the booth seat next to him. "I wanted you to have these," he said nervously. "I wanted to thank you for the chat at the park the other day."

Andrea's heart started to pound; chat at the park? It seemed she vaguely remembered talking to some guy, but had this man been him? She couldn't tell; all she really remembered was that the man at Gooseneck Park wore a cowboy hat, and she definitely didn't recall him having eyes like this.

He was still holding out the flowers, his hand trembling. Jason's cowboy hat sat on the seat next to him, unnoticed. How did he know where she worked? She was sure she hadn't told him that! Was he some kind of stalker? Had this strange guy been following her or something?

"Um, I'm not sure…"

Jason set the flowers down on the table, suddenly realizing that she didn't remember him. "I shared chips with your little Millie. You got all nervous and ran off. I hope it wasn't me who made you feel that way, especially since you had to deal with that guy…"

Andrea's eyes grew wide. "What guy?"

Now Jason was getting nervous; Andrea seemed a bit perturbed with him. He began to panic, his heart pounding. "I wanted to make sure you were okay—"

He stopped; she was just staring at him, mouth open. He was! The guy was a stalker! What? Did she only have the capacity to attract freaks?

Andrea hesitated. "Uh, you know, I think someone else should serve you tonight. Do you even know how weird you sound, telling me about meeting me in the park and then following me home?"

"Andrea, wait—"

Now she got really anxious. "Did you just call me by my first name? How do you know my first name?"

A smile flickered at the corner of Jason's mouth. "Because it's on your nametag? I mean, you told me at the park, but it's on your nametag too."

She had enough; no matter what he said, she saw him as just another one of them. They always had their paws and tongues out, and when you got too close, they bit. She couldn't even cross the room without someone hitting on her! Andrea smirked, shook her head, and plopped down in the booth across from him. She could feel other customers watching, and she could hear their silence as they tried to eavesdrop.

"You know what, Mister?" she began. "You are just one of several who have contributed to making my day horrible. I can't take an order, bring a meal, or even get a decent sleep at night because of men just like you, just like all of you!" Andrea paused and cast a long look around the dining room; tears were welling up in her eyes, threatening to fall, but she didn't care. "So, why don't you take your psycho stalking butt to a strip club or something, where you'll likely bat a thousand, because you're never going to get anywhere with me!"

She jumped up and ran to the back without another word or thought. Yes, she had just lost complete control and gone off on some strange guy with wildflowers, but for Pete's sake, couldn't they just let her be? Couldn't they simply give her five-minutes time in her life to breathe?

Andrea reached the small cubby station that housed all the lockers. She plopped down on a stool situated on the far end of the station, buried her face in her hands, and cried. How could she be so tired and still function? It was obvious, even to her, that she needed rest, and she needed time away from men.

"Are you okay? What happened out there?"

Andrea looked up, swiping at her face with the backs of her hands as she did. Dana stood there, a sad look on her face, and her forehead wrought with concern. Sniffling, Andrea gave an exasperated, sarcastic smile and shrugged.

"He's only the hundredth man I've had to deal with today," she muttered. "I'm tired, but I can't afford to miss work."

Dana nodded. "Well, I apologized to him for you, then suggested he get a taco or something… like, someplace else. Take an hour, Andrea; order some food or something. Get yourself together then hit the floor again, okay?"

Andrea agreed. Dana was pretty wise for a woman who could be so brassy sometimes. She felt deep affection for her boss and was grateful that the down-to-earth woman came from a place in life that allowed her to understand bad men and all they were made of.

That was one thing Andrea was getting to know too well: almost all of them were dirtballs, and there was nothing she could do about it but protect herself.

∞

Chesterfield... 5 miles

Jason punched the gas even harder than he had been hitting it, taking the speed of the pickup to eighty. It felt good to fly down the road, windows down and hot breeze rushing through the cab of the truck. Brahms pumped through the speakers' full blast, pleasantly numbing his pain. Jason had never been so embarrassed and humiliated in his life, short of the war.

He covered the short distance to town in no time. Soon, he was merging from concrete to gravel as he pulled into the driveway leading home. The 'Brandtley Ranch' sign that hung over the entrance of the drive was swaying pretty hard in the wind, but Jason took no real notice of it; he was still in shock.

Jason pulled the truck up to the front of the house and turned off the ignition. He pressed his forehead against the backs of his hands as they gripped the steering wheel and focused on breathing. As he calmed, he chastised himself for driving when he was so furious.

Five minutes passed, then ten. His mind was whirling around the situation at the Cozy Cowboy; he replayed the entire scene, word for word, over and over in his mind. Each time, he picked up on something that softened his heart more and more.

Her face had been so evil-looking, and her voice so angry, yet, she had a tear in her eye. Andrea had referred to all of you. It wasn't just him, it was men in general. Jason remembered the confrontation he had witnessed from behind the lilac bushes at Gooseneck Park, the confrontation with that guy, and the neighbor with the gun. The more he thought about it, the easier it was to convince himself that her reaction and attitude were due to the stressors in her life right then; it wasn't him personally at all.

It was also her expressions, voice, and attitude that he found himself despising. If she was able to react that way under job pressure, then she was capable of it when life was good. He would have to think on that particular observation; it was too soon to determine if she was just a pain in the neck sometimes, or not.

How could he fix this? How could he let her know that he was sorry if it had been a bad time? Jason didn't want to harm her; he just wanted to get to know her, to possibly be her friend. If it was meant to be, and he thought it was, it would blossom on its own.

Now his mind went to how he must have looked, sitting there in that booth with a sad puppy-dog expression on his face, and rejected wildflowers sitting on the table before him. A nervous, heartbroken wreck,

Jason paced around the house until well after midnight.

Jason lay down on the couch, remote control in hand, and surfed through television channels until he fell asleep.

∞

Wait! That was it! The wildflowers!

That was how he would apologize, that was how he would try to break the ice for a second time! He would send her a bouquet of the exact wildflowers, and he would include a card consisting of heartfelt apologies and a simple request for friendship. She seemed to be a tough case, a girl who had suffered a few hard knocks. Jason was stubborn, too; he wouldn't give up so easily.

So, Jason was sitting home alone on the ranch, nursing his wounded pride and placing an order with Fancy Florist in Cheyenne. "Why don't you include a box of chocolate with that please?" He wanted them to attempt delivery to two locations: first, the Cozy Cowboy; if she wasn't there, they were to deliver at her home address. He dictated what the card was to read while the florist wrote it down for him.

Andrea,

I am sorry you had a bad day; I sincerely apologize if I played a part in making it worse.

Please forgive me, I hope that we can be friends. I wish the best for you.

Hopeful,

Jason Brandtley

He had written the note down ahead of time, before calling the florist. After he hung up with the man, he reread it several times. Was it too cheesy? Would she even care? Or would his effort do nothing more than piss her off even worse? He thought about canceling the flowers for a fraction of a second, then remembered that he'd used his bank card; the order was placed.

He thought about everything yet again, then it hit him that he wouldn't even know if she got the flowers unless she called him, and he hadn't included his number. There was only one way to find out, and he didn't have to think about it twice: he would have to drive to Cheyenne in the morning, sort of hanging out and watching. There was nothing wrong with that, was there? He wanted to see her face when she got the flowers.

CHAPTER 8

Today was one of the busiest days of the week at
The Cozy Cowboy. There were always the regulars, but
today also welcomed a rush and a steady stream of
brunch buffet fans who wouldn't miss it for the world.
Usually, Andrea's presence at the restaurant was a given;
if she wasn't there, people actually worried. But today
was different; Dana ordered her to take a day off,
promising she could make it up by staying over a couple
hours at a time here and there.

It was the first day in nearly two years that Andrea
didn't go to work, and the only thing she could think
about was the tips she was missing.

Andrea didn't know what to do with herself. Her
small, one-bedroom apartment was spotless, and
laundry was done. She had taken Millie outside three
times already, and it wasn't even noon. Sure, she had
slept soundly and woke refreshed, but now she was on
the verge of losing her mind.

She found a movie that she hadn't seen in a long
time, and she was settling in to watch it with a burrito
and some apple juice when her cell phone chirped.
Andrea groaned, burrito half-way to her mouth, and

glanced down at the smartphone screen: it was work. Certainly, Dana wouldn't demand that she take the day off and then call her in.

"Hello?" she answered.

Dana cleared her throat. "Hey, girl. How are you feeling?"

"Better, since I got a good night's sleep," she replied. "Do you need me to come in?"

Dana chuckled "Absolutely not... nice try, though. I just wanted to give you a heads-up. First, Brad called and asked if you were working. I told him you were busy and couldn't come to the phone. I told him if he calls again, and I get wind of it, I'll get a restraining order myself. He hung up."

Andrea couldn't help but smile; Dana could be a bit imposing sometimes, and she was afraid of no one. "Thank you; sorry he's such a jerk."

"No prob. Now, number two: Fancy Florist brought some flowers for you, but I told them you weren't here." Dana coughed a couple of times. "I should tell you, I thought they were from Brad, so I looked at the card. They were from Jason."

Andrea creased her brow; was that the guy from yesterday, the guy from the park? She couldn't remember his name, and she was almost sure he hadn't told it to her yesterday. Her brain almost hurt from straining to remember.

"I think that was the customer I blew up on," Andrea finally replied.

"Yes," Dana replied.

"Did you take the flowers?"

"Nah." Dana was beginning to sound impatient. "I tried, but they said they had an alternate delivery address and mentioned your street, so I'd be expecting them. Look, honey, I gotta go; we just got a party of ten."

Dana immediately disconnected, leaving Andrea sitting there, staring at the phone and smiling. After a moment, she pushed play and returned to her movie and gave the burrito her full attention. Unless that delivery person showed up, nothing could stop her now.

Suddenly a buzzing sound filled the air.

The burrito had been less than an inch from her face when the buzzer to the security door went off. Someone was there, and she wasn't surprised. Andrea wished she could see out front so she could make sure it wasn't that stupid Brad. She wished she had never gotten mixed up with him.

She pushed the button on the call box. "Yes?"

"I have a delivery for Andrea Harder. It's Fancy Florists."

Andrea let go of the button and groaned. So, Dana hadn't imagined it. Man, whoever this guy was who sent the flowers, she was sure it was the guy from the park, and he was really starting to creep her out.

She left the apartment, closing the door on Millie after reassuring her that she would be right back. Before she even got to the door, she could see the delivery man, a young man with a bushy mustache. He had a bored look on his face, and Andrea could see that he was tapping his foot. Reaching the door, she grasped the handle and swung it wide.

"I'm Andrea Harder."

The man's boredom was instantly replaced with a broad smile. "Miss Harder, have a beautiful day! Greetings from your admirer and from Fancy Florists!"

Before she could even think to respond, the man thrust the bouquet into her surprised arms along with a box of chocolates, and walked off, heading for a green truck with the Fancy Florists logo on the side. She started to stop him so she could make him take the flowers with him, but then thought twice, chocolate. No, she could deal with the flowers herself.

Andrea paused and looked at the small envelope, which simply read 'Andrea.'

Still standing in the doorway, she fished the small card out of the envelope and read the simple message inside. Signed 'Hopeful, Jason Brandtley.' Jason Brandtley… she vaguely remembered that as being the name of the guy in the park; it was him all right. He had said something about coming into a farm or ranch of some kind, hadn't he?"

Andrea shrugged and stepped away from the security door, pausing to make sure the latch caught properly. As she walked back to her apartment, she studied the flowers: wildflowers, just like those he had tried to give her in the restaurant the day before. He had apologized in the card, and it sounded very sweet, but she didn't really register that at all. The thing on her mind was the fact that this guy knew where she worked, and he knew where she lived as well, even her apartment number! The realization gave her goosebumps.

No sooner had she closed her apartment door after entering than her cell rang yet again. A quick look at the screen told her it was Brad. The guy just wouldn't give up, would he?

With a shake of her head, she answered her cell as she walked.

"Andrea, please don't hang up."

Brad greeted her immediately with those words. She didn't even bother to get upset; the guy had been told, over and over again. More than likely she would have to use her lunch break the following day to obtain an order of protection from the courthouse with his name on it.

"What now, Brad?" Her voice was weary.

He was still for a moment, but she could hear him breathing. At last, he said, simply, "Don't get upset; I get it… we're through. It was hard to accept because I really like you. But it is what it is, and I'm sorry I've put you through so much grief."

Andrea listened patiently. She could hear the sound of a bar in the background, and she figured he was at the Watering Hole up the street. But he didn't sound intoxicated, which was the primary reason she didn't hang up the line.

"I appreciate that," she replied at last. "I never wanted to hurt you; I just don't think we are the right people for each other."

Brad made noises of agreement. "Like I said, I get it. Which leads me to the reason for calling. I left a couple of t-shirts there, and you know me… I don't want to lose them. Can I just swing by and grab them?"

Immediately, Andrea thought of exactly which t-shirts he was referring to, and she was kicking herself in the bum for not giving them to him yesterday. Yes, she knew him well enough to know that, but she also knew he likely left them at her house on purpose, just to have a reason to call if she ever broke it off. Those shirts had been there for months!

"Brad, I really don't feel comfortable with you stopping by," she said slowly, careful not to get him all worked up. "I mean, with the breakup and all, it just makes it more difficult. Um, where are you?"

He didn't sound upset at all when he answered. "You're right. I'm at the Hole. Maybe you could walk them down? I'll buy you a beer."

Andrea sighed. "Thanks, but I'll pass; I'm not feeling too well. I'll be down in a half-hour, but I'm not staying, Brad."

"I understand," he said, his voice filled with resignation. "I knew you weren't at work like that fat chick told me when I called. I was sitting outside at the time."

"Brad, look…"

He interrupted her. "No, wait. I'm sorry. Okay, I'll see you in a half-hour, no beer, and you're not staying, I know."

"Thank you," she mumbled flatly, then she hung up.

Andrea let her arm drop to the side and looked around her apartment, exasperated. Millie sat on the arm of the sofa, staring up at her mistress, so she smiled at the little dog. The poor fur baby couldn't catch a break and have a whole day with Mom, could she?

She walked into her room and knelt before the dresser, then proceeded to fish two t-shirts out of the bottom drawer. After looking them over to make sure she had the right ones, Andrea refolded them and took them to the kitchen, where she put them into a plastic sack.

"Wanna take a walk, Mill?"

The dog jumped from the couch and let Andrea put on her leash. Grabbing her cell phone and house keys, she left the apartment, locking it up behind her.

R.W.K. Clark

CHAPTER 9

Jason was watching Andrea when she got the bouquet, and he was watching when she read the card. It was frustrating to him because the look on her face did nothing to give away her emotional reaction to the friendly gift. She had simply read it and went back inside of the apartment building without so much as a glance at her surroundings.

He had been parked directly across the street. In his mind, he had imagined that she would read the card and look around, her blue eyes seeking out his brown ones. She would spot him and break into a huge smile, then run across the street to him and fall into his arms.

Now he simply sat there with a heavy heart, not really hearing the beauty of Beethoven as it poured into the cab of his truck. He couldn't even snap back to reality and drive away because he was too busy replaying the flower scene over and over in his mind, trying to figure out if she had really shown any sign of excitement or happiness; he could remember none.

He wanted to be sick. Jason couldn't think of any more options that might get Andrea Harder's attention. As far as he was concerned, there was nothing more for him to try to do. It hurt mostly because he really had his hopes up, and now his hopes were dashed.

Reaching for the ignition, Jason decided it was time to go. Just as he took hold of the keys, something caught his eye to the far right. Slowly, Jason turned his head just in time to see Andrea coming out of her apartment building, Millie on her leash running out in front of her.

He held his breath as though he was afraid she would hear it, but from what he could tell, Andrea took no notice of his presence at all. She simply started walking up the street, seemingly oblivious to all that was around her. In her right hand, she held Millie's leash, and in the other, a plastic sack. Andrea was walking in the opposite direction of the avenue; he had no idea where she could be going.

I'll follow her, he thought. I'll stay far enough behind that she won't notice me, but I'll keep her in sight, just to be sure she's okay. He managed to turn on the ignition with shaking hands, but he couldn't pull his eyes away from the angel walking down the street; just watching her made his heart skip a beat.

Andrea reached a corner, then crossed the street, allowing Millie to stop on the other side. Jason stayed against the curb, pulling out after the dog had finished her business.

She crossed another street, then continued on. So far, she hadn't looked back even one time. Why was that, Jason wondered. Wasn't she at all concerned about the idiot who had been hassling her outside her building the other day? What if he was the one driving the truck? She should be more careful, and once he had gained her trust, he would talk to her about that.

The pretty strawberry blonde crossed another street, then went halfway down the block and stopped right in front of a bar called The Watering Hole. Andrea opened the door, stuck her head inside, and then stepped back and let the door swing shut. Of course, Jason thought. She couldn't go into the establishment with Millie; she was there to see someone and for no other reason.

Jason didn't have to wonder who she saw for long. In seconds, the door opened and the big dirtball from the other day stepped outside. He greeted her, standing straight so he could show off his broad shoulders as he did so. The guy tried to hug Andrea next, but she dodged him and held out the plastic bag. Jason could tell that he was pissed that she rejected his embrace.

He sidled the truck over to the curb and gently put it in park; Jason was concerned that she would turn around and see him, but then he remembered that she had never seen his truck. He rolled his window half-way down, shut off the ignition, then sat back to watch the couple.

Brad didn't take the bag that Andrea was holding out. He stared at it, then smirked. "Well, thanks for bringing my shirts. I thought, since you are here, maybe we could have just one beer together, but I see you have Millie."

"Yeah, I have a bunch of stuff to do today, so I really don't have time," she replied. She was keeping her distance from him, standing back and even looking around, as though everything else was more interesting than he was.

The guy chuckled and shook his head. "You can't even see fit to give me the time of day, can you?" He asked sarcastically, taking a couple of steps toward her. "Is this what you did to the other guys you dated? Made them fall in love with you, then sent them packing? You know what, Andrea? I'm not going to be just another notch on your belt, lady."

He took another step in her direction, making Millie yap a couple of times at him. Jason's hand went for the door handle of the truck but stopped when he saw her backing away. The guy didn't advance again, so he waited to get out. Maybe he wouldn't need to interfere.

Andrea shook her head sadly. "I should have known there was more to me coming than just to bring you t-shirts. Look, I really have to go."

She began to walk away, but Brad grabbed her arm and jerked her back to him. Andrea let out a yelp and yanked the arm back; immediately, Jason could see the anger come over the guy's face. He drew back and swung his arm, striking Andrea on the cheek with the back of his hand and knocking her to the ground.

Millie started to go nuts, and Brad instantly looked worried. He jerked the bag from the ground and looked around the area, missing Jason's presence. Then he rushed into the bar, muttering something about Andrea, that he was through with her mind games. As he disappeared into the dark interior of the establishment,

Jason turned his focus to her; she was sitting on the ground with Millie's leash in one hand. Her other hand was holding her cheek, and from where he was sitting, he could see a tear fall down her cheek.

Jason didn't even think about what he was going to do next; he was instantly on autopilot. Flinging the truck door open, he jumped from the cab and headed for her, not even bothering to close the door behind him. He rushed across the street, his head and heart filled with concern for the beautiful young lady sitting on the sidewalk, crying.

He had nearly reached her when she turned and saw him. But instead of her expression being one of relief, Andrea's face appeared to convey nothing but shock. Her hand dropped from her cheek, her mouth fell open, and she began to struggle to stand up before he could get to her.

She began to back away from him, jerking Millie's leash as she did so. "What are you doing here? Why are you following me around? Help! Help!" she screamed.

"No, wait… I just…"

The bar door flew open and out came Brad; he was accompanied by two other men, both scraggly-looking with rheumy eyes. Jason stopped running, his hand in the air. The one thing he really took note of was the look on the guy's face: both his mouth, and his eyes, were smiling. Inwardly, Jason groaned; he knew what was coming before it even hit him.

"Brad, don't!"

That was the last thing that Jason was actually aware

of hearing. Brad ran at him, full-speed and hit him in the midsection like a linebacker sacking a quarterback. All of the air left his lungs at once as he flew backward, airborne, with Brad still wrapped around him. Jason barely even felt it when his back slammed against the concrete of the street. With no breath in his lungs, he was helpless, only able to lie on the ground in a fetal position while Brad pummeled his entire body, from head to toe.

He felt every blow, yet he felt none of them at all. Jason was aware of the taste of blood in his mouth and ringing in his ears. Punches and kicks continued to come, faster than he could register; he could do nothing to get the upper hand or get on his feet. He was helpless. Finally, Brad delivered a severe kick to Jason's stomach, and vomit shot from his mouth and puddled on the street next to his head.

Brad began to laugh. "That'll teach you." He was breathing heavily, and from the slits of his eyes, Jason could see that the guy was still smiling as well. "Thank you for the entertainment; I needed to get a bit of aggression out, punk." With that, he spat at Jason, the wad of saliva slapping the pavement right next to his head; he winced in disgust and tightened his arms around his stomach. Jason still couldn't breathe.

He lay there and watched the three men return to the bar. Andrea was gone; he heard the bully ask where she went, but he couldn't hear the reply of the other men. Once he was sure they were back inside, Jason began to struggle his way back to his feet. It was still difficult to catch his breath; he seemed to hurt all over.

When he reached his truck, he glanced back at the bar and saw that a couple of raggedy women were gawking at him through the glass door. Mentally waving them off, he climbed into the vehicle and closed the door as best as he could. He just wanted to get out of there, then he would survey the damage. For now, his pain and humiliation were enough motivation to start the truck and get it moving. The only thing he noted was the blood all over his face, which he caught a glimpse of when he checked behind him in the rearview mirror before pulling the truck away from the curb.

As he drove away, it all struck him as funny, but not the good kind of funny. Jason began to laugh, slightly at first, but within a couple of blocks, he was roaring.

Unbeknownst to Jason Brandtley, Andrea and Brad had pushed him over the edge.

R.W.K. Clark

CHAPTER 10

Jason sat in silence on the sofa, an ice pack pressed against a deep cut on his left cheekbone. The television was on some show, but he had no idea what it was; he even had the volume turned down. Instead, Jason listened to Mozart's 'Suite in C Major'; it made more sense to him than the drama on the television screen.

He was calm now, but when he first left The Watering Hole, he was nearly in hysterics. The anger wasn't gone; oh no, he was still enraged like he had never been before. But instead of laughing like crazy, or screaming and breaking things, Jason was serene and smiling. As for the rage, well, it was definitely directed at someone. Truth be told, it had nothing to do with Brad.

He was pissed at Andrea Harder. He had never met such a rude human being in his life. Since meeting her, Jason had done nothing but dwell fondly on her existence and daydream of her beautiful face. He had spent money on flowers and travel, and he had overlooked her hostility when she embarrassed him at The Cozy Cowboy. Now, here he was, beat and bleeding, all because he had tried to help her. He stood up for her when her former beau got physical and hit her. What did he get in return? He got beat to a pulp, that's what he got.

He had come home and gotten cleaned up. Now, he simply sat in the same place and position he had been sitting in since returning, holding the freezing pack to his throbbing face and thinking how he was going to deal with the situation. Sure, he could just let it go and move on; that would be the smart thing to do. But he just couldn't relent, and he knew it. Didn't that girl's upbringing teach her how to be decent and kind to anyone? Not that anyone deserved to be hit or beaten, but perhaps this was the same behavior she had demonstrated to that Brad guy, and that was the reason for his hostility. If that was the case, and Jason believed it was, then he felt a responsibility, an obligation, to teach little Miss Andrea Harder some kind of lesson.

Women… they were all the same. Except for his mother, Signe, anyway. How could he have been so blindsided by Andrea's resemblance to the woman in her younger years? Her personality was nothing like his Mom's; she had been gentle, generous, and kind. Andrea was harsh, painful, and obnoxious.

Now a smile came over his face, accompanying the wince that he brought out by shifting the ice pack. The facts, for him, were simple; he cared far too much about Andrea and the outcome of her life to just let things go. No, Jason wouldn't just curl up in a corner and forget about his hopes of being with her. Jason intended to go the extra mile, just as he always had in life.

Jason was going to teach her a lesson.

Even now, as he sat there on that sofa, he had a plan, and a wonderful plan it was. Not only would Jason separate her from all the chaos her life was made up of, but he would also spend each and every day tending to her needs, getting to know her, and letting her get to know him. Now, he wasn't foolish. He knew that if he approached her and asked her to come to the ranch willingly, she would laugh in his face if she didn't call a cop. No, she wouldn't cooperate. He would have to take extreme measures.

He would abduct her, plain and simple.

Where would he keep her? Oh, he hadn't overlooked that at all. First thing in the morning, he would take a trip to Ranch Supply. There, he would purchase everything needed to construct her new home. It would be cozy, stylish, and very comfortable, with all the luxuries of home. It wouldn't be 'home'; but it would be a place for her to live at the far end of the basement, caged like the animal she chose to act like. He didn't intend to hurt her in any way, but it was definitely his intention to straighten her attitude. She needed to learn some manners and compassion; she needed to learn how to be a decent human being. Until she did, she didn't deserve to live the life of freedom that soldiers fought for. In her current state, as far as he was concerned, she behaved no better than the terrorists that held him in the metal box.

A glance at the clock told him it was nearly midnight. He stood up, took the ice pack back to the freezer, and changed it out for a fresh one. Next, Jason made his way down to the basement to get a good look around.

The basement was massive, twice as large as the house itself. His father had told him once when he was younger that there had been another house standing where this one stood, but a bit further south. The back part of the basement had been original to that house; the front part had been constructed as part of the new one. Both of them now coexisted together.

He stopped at the bottom of the basement stairs and looked around, still smiling. A large window near the ceiling lit the room. Thick blue carpeting covered the floor, and black overstuffed furniture was set up around the room. There was a fireplace in this section, a large flat screen that he hadn't used since he'd been home, and a stereo system with surround sound. At the far end of the room, there was a large break in the wall that measured six-feet high and six-feet across; to walk through it meant you were heading to the back section of the basement. Jason crossed the room, then stepped over the threshold into that section.

This part was about the same size as the first, with a few differences. It, too, was carpeted in blue shag, but there were no windows whatsoever. In the corner were a toilet, sink, and standing shower. His mother had separated it from the rest of the area with simple paneling, but for his plans that wouldn't do; he couldn't run the risk of Andrea living down here in captivity and tearing walls out. He would do it himself and replace the paneling with nice, colorful curtains so she could have privacy.

Aside from those things, the large room was empty, but in his mind's eye, it was fully furnished. He would create a living area and separate sleeping area. She wouldn't need a kitchen, because he'd be bringing her meals and whatever else she needed. He would also make sure she had plenty of nice, new clothes, as well as all appropriate hygiene items. He would decorate and give her plants. If she learned to behave herself, he would also make sure that she had Millie as well.

As for the large open entrance to the area, Jason had a solution for that, too. He would install large iron bars, the kind that jail cells were made of. The only way out of the cell would be with a key, or by changing her attitude. It would be then, and only then that Jason would even consider letting her back into the real world. He didn't care about consequences, not at this point. All he cared about now was bringing her here. He looked around the large empty space one more time, smiled, and flipped off the light before heading back upstairs. He had a lot of planning to do; right now, he would make a list of all the things he would need to create Andrea Harder's new home.

Not only would he need furnishings, clothing, and other necessities for building, he would need new speakers and wire. Jason intended to make sure that his beautiful, calming classical music pumped through the entire basement at all times. It would soothe her the way it soothed him, and it would help her transition go much, much easier. There was absolutely no way she would be able to fight its transforming power for very long.

He was up until dawn finishing the list, even double and triple checking it to his satisfaction. When at last the sun began to rise, the soreness and stinging that had been inflicted upon him were forgotten. Jason was able to go out and take care of Winnie and Rayne, feeding them and making sure that Winnie got any pain medication she needed.

He was going to have to get a bit more of that, too. If Andrea were half the fighter he thought she was, Jason would have to utilize the medications to keep her under control, at least initially. He would definitely have to use something to subdue her in the beginning.

When he was finished with the horses, he showered and dressed, then headed for Ranch Supply, whistling with happiness the entire time.

∞

The entire next two weeks were very busy, both for Jason and Andrea, in their respective lives.

Jason did nothing but focus on reconstructing the back half of the basement and taking care of the horses. He was thankful for Kirk Hampton, the man who tended the sheep. He knew that, without the man, he wouldn't be able to accomplish the goal he was aiming for at all. Jason made it a point to talk to the man; it certainly wouldn't do to raise suspicions of any kind at this point.

So, he worked from sunup to sundown on the new room, drilling, cutting, sawing, installing. He listened to classical music, and he went about his work with peace and happiness; he was doing the right thing. It was right for him, and it would be right for Andrea. Maybe she wouldn't understand it clearly at first, but before it was over, she would. Of that, Jason Brandtley was confident.

As for Andrea, she all but forgot that Jason even existed. As soon as Brad started to administer his beating, she had run off, putting all thoughts of him behind her. Jason was just another one of the men who tried to get down her pants, another one who saw her as nothing more than a piece of meat.

She picked up extra shifts, worked overtime, and focused on putting her life in order. Brad had tried to call her a couple of times after the incident at The Watering Hole, playing the 'protection' card. Hadn't he proved his love? Wasn't he the only one who had? Instead of entertaining his fantasies, Andrea simply ignored his calls, refusing to return them. By the time a week had passed, she had realized she hadn't heard from him, or seen him, in days, and she was able to breathe a bit easier.

On a few occasions, mostly while she worked or tried to sleep, thoughts of the strange guy from the park shot through her mind. Had he been okay? Why didn't she try to help? As a matter of fact, why hadn't she at least been a bit nicer to him? As she considered the beating he took, she thought she might have misread him approaching her outside the bar that day. Guilt would come, and that was when she would push it all away. He shouldn't have been stalking her at all.

Two-weeks since the scene outside the Hole, she lay in bed drifting off peacefully. In the split-second, before she dozed off, a picture of the stranger from the park came to her mind; he was curled up on the ground, taking kicks from Brad. Like all the rest of her thoughts of him, she pushed it out of her mind and fell asleep.

CHAPTER 11

Jason sat in his truck sipping a cup of hot coffee. It was six in the morning, but he had been awake for hours. Today was the day, and he needed to be on alert to make everything perfect. Yes, today was the day that he brought Andrea home, and back to her senses.

He was watching her building from a block away. Since she had gotten a good look at his truck the day Brad attacked him, he didn't want to risk being spotted. He also had no idea what her schedule was for the day, but if she stayed true to form, it would consist of nothing but work. It seems her entire life revolved around the Cozy Cowboy and making money. Well, after today, money would be the least of her worries.

He saw her bedroom light come on; Andrea was awake. Jason smiled and took another sip of his coffee, reveling in its bitter warmth as he kept his eyes on the window. Her shadow passed by, then reappeared as she put on a bathrobe; Andrea was getting ready to shower for the day.

Once she was out of sight again, he leaned over and reached for a small cooler that was on the passenger seat. He flipped open the lid and looked inside, just as he had already done ten times. Nestled inside, wrapped in a handkerchief, were two syringes. Not lethal doses, but doses appropriate, and strong enough, for a female human being of her size. The perfect drug to subdue her, making it easy for him to overpower her and get her into the truck. He was thankful for his king cab, if for no other reason than this one. A glance over his shoulder at the bed he had made behind the seat comforted him. She would be fine back there, all the way home to Chesterfield; he was confident she wouldn't make a peep.

Jason also had a bag of Ruff Snacks for Millie. Hopefully, the dog didn't put up too much of a fit when he grabbed Andrea. He fully intended to take the dog with them to his home; Millie would make a great motivating factor for Andrea to buck up and change her ways.

Since he didn't know what her work schedule was, time-wise, it would be hit or miss. He assumed her schedule was somewhat erratic; after all, she was a waitress at a greasy spoon.

After about ten minutes, Andrea's shadow appeared in front of the window again, this time with a towel wrapped around her head. He thought about tonight, the night he would take her. The other times he had come, she had worked until the café closed. Money was tight for her, he was sure, so he trusted that she would work until closing time again. It would be then after she came home and took Millie for a walk that he would snatch her up. If she ended up getting off earlier, he would simply wait patiently for the last walk of the day, because this 'deed' had to be done at night.

Kirk Hampton was going to look in on the horses today, though Jason had seen to it that they had plenty of food and water. It was mostly Winnie's pain that he was worried about; he dosed her up pretty good before he left, and he had let Kirk know that. The guy wasn't at all familiar with horses or medication injections. All Jason could do was hope that she would be fine until he was able to get home.

He kept his eyes on her shadow, watching her dress and brush her hair until she turned off the bedroom light and disappeared from sight. Draining his coffee, he braced himself for her departure. At seven, she came out with the dog and waited while Millie did her business. By seven-thirty, she was walking up the street, purse over her shoulder and jacket on. Andrea walked to work that much he had figured out on his own, and it made his plan much easier to execute.

She strolled with a carefree step, a cheerful look on her face. Jason thought about what it would be like living with her, eating meals together, talking late into the night. He could hardly wait for tonight when he would put her in the truck and took her home; it would be heaven.

As he watched her making her way up the street, his heart skipped a beat. Yes, he was in love with her, he could admit it. His heart skipped several beats as he followed her with his eyes. Jason was at the point that he knew she would likely never be his, but none of this was about that. It wasn't about relationships or sex, or even control. No, it wasn't about any of those things. It was about teaching rude little Andrea Harder to act like a human being.

∞

Today was going to be a warm one. Andrea wasn't even to the avenue yet, and she already regretted her decision to bring a jacket. She paused long enough to remove the garment and sling it over her shoulder, then continued walking to the Cozy Cowboy. The place was already bustling, which was somewhat surprising. Usually, it was just the regulars that made appearances on weekday mornings.

She was just getting ready to open the entrance door to the café when a truck caught her eye. Spinning her head around, she tried to get a clearer look, but it turned left and out of sight. Where did she know that truck from? Andrea stood there, door ajar, trying to recollect having seen it before. With a shrug, she gave up and went inside; must belong to a regular or something.

Andrea was greeted by several dirtbags as soon as she walked into the main dining room, which distracted her completely from any thoughts she had about vehicles outside. Time to get busy; it looked to her like the two girls who were there were a bit overwhelmed already.

CHAPTER 12

Jason sat in the parking lot waiting for any sign that the Cozy Cowboy was getting ready to close. Cars continued to pull into the lot in a fairly steady stream, telling him that he was getting his hopes up a bit too early. From where he sat with his fresh coffee, Jason could see Andrea, and she didn't look like she was concerned with the clock quite yet.

His CD player soothed him with Tchaikovsky, and he found it to be more than grounding. He had been filled with anxiety an hour before, which influenced his decision to turn the player back on. Why had he even considered turning it off? This music seemed to be the one thing that kept him on the level anymore. He certainly hoped that Andrea felt the same way after he turned her on to it.

The next thought that came to his mind concerned the décor, furnishings, and personal possessions that he had purchased when he set up her new 'home.' Jason found himself smiling; he hoped Andrea liked everything, and he hoped she would be comfortable. He wanted to believe in his heart that he had just experienced her bad side because of all the pressure that prick of a man was putting on her, but he had a feeling that she tended to be rude and hostile anyway. Was he doing the right thing? Was all the work he had put into the basement really worth it?

Yes, he was sure it was.

Nocturnes by Chopin began playing, verifying his thoughts and feelings. Yes, this was the right thing to do, and the timing of this particular piece coming on was proof. It was one of Jason's favorites, after all, but if he were honest, he would have to admit that he had many favorites, some he had even forgotten and wouldn't recall them until he heard them again.

He lifted his coffee cup to his lips, then shook it; it was empty. When had he even managed to drink it? Jason couldn't recall taking so much as a sip. Turning his attention back to the large window at The Cozy Cowboy, he noted that Andrea was making her way toward a booth with a large tray of food; he wouldn't miss much if he hopped over to the gas station across the street from the lot he was in. He would even be able to watch her the entire time he walked.

So, he did; he watched her while he walked, kept his eyes on her the entire time he paid for his beverage, and focused on Andrea as he walked back to his truck. Soon, Jason was settling back into his truck, adjusting the volume on the Chopin tune, which he had been able to replay with a simple push of the button.

It was now almost 8:15. Soon, Jason would be picking up the pretty strawberry blonde who was now helping a young man bus a table. Soon, he would take her to her new home, and Jason would be able to show her all of the furniture and pretty clothes he bought for her. He didn't expect her to be happy about any of it, not immediately, anyway. No, she was going to be furious, but it wasn't going to make a difference. Andrea Harder wasn't going to be going anywhere until she changed her attitude, no matter how long that took.

He was patient; he was equipped. He had a long, but necessary, process to go through with her. But Jason Brandtley was well-prepared, and he had all the time in the world.

Andrea placed the dirty glasses in a strategic pattern around the plates on the tray: best to have as much balance as possible when carrying that kind of weight. A backward glance told her that the busser had disappeared into the kitchen with the other plates and glasses. This had been a big table, and they had left her a great tip: a full thirty-percent. With a slight smile, Andrea pushed her hair out of her face with the back of her hand and gently hoisted up the tray and headed for the kitchen herself.

It was five minutes to ten. She had made it through another back-breaking double shift alive. Now she just had two tables left, and they were wrapping up their meals as she spoke. All she had to do was clean up after them, take care of her side work, and she would be heading home herself.

A flash of thought regarding Brad came into her mind as she unloaded the tray at the dishwashing station. What a relief that he had seemingly given up!

The thought of going home might spark a bit of apprehension in her heart, but Andrea was sure that it was all going to be fine; she hadn't heard from him in days.

By the time she headed back out to the dining room, Dana was settling checks for the last two tables. While her boss made jokes with the customers, Andrea began to bus the remaining tables, happy that she would soon be walking out the door for the night. All she had to do was put the salad bar items away, vacuum, and check out so she could get her tips. They would be easy enough tasks that she could probably do with her eyes closed; freedom was imminent.

"Wow, you've had a good night, Andrea." Dana was finally cashing her out; the busboy was gone, and the lights were down for the night. "Can I give you a lift home?" the woman asked as she handed over Andrea's tips.

She shook her head. "Since Brad's been laying off, I have been enjoying my walking time. Besides, it's just a few blocks, and it's a beautiful night."

Dana smiled. "So, I guess I'll see you tomorrow afternoon. What are you going to do with yourself, having a morning off?"

"I'm taking Millie to the dog park," Andrea replied with a wink. "She has a Yorkie pal there who I think she might be getting a little serious with!"

She stepped out into the night, putting her bag and jacket over her shoulder while Dana locked up. With one more wave, Andrea walked away in the direction of her apartment. Dana continued to look after her until she was out of sight; for some reason, the business owner had a deep, unsettling feeling.

"I sure hope you're right about that dirtball, Brad," she muttered to herself before making her way to her office to settle the books for the night.

It was a beautiful night, with a nice, warm wind blowing, and a sky so clear that the stars could easily be counted. Andrea frequently gazed up at the sky as she strolled, taking no notice of anything or anyone around her, including the large truck that pulled out just as she passed. She was so enraptured by the feeling of a hard day's work, coupled with the perfection of the evening that she didn't take note of the truck, waiting for her to turn off the avenue onto her street.

Before long, Andrea stood on her stoop, fishing her keys out of her bag. As she felt around in the dim lighting of the porch, the truck, now with its lights off, slowly coasted alongside the curb, stopping short about twenty feet from her place and killing the ignition.

Jason watched her as her hand groped around blindly in her purse. He peered through the darkness as she put the key into the lock and then disappeared into the security building. Soon, he knew, she would come back out and take her dog out to walk; at this time of night, Jason was confident she would do all of this in the backyard area of the complex. Jason started the truck again, pulled away from the curb, and drove up to the next corner, where he took a left. Next, he took another left into the alley that ran behind her building, and he parked the vehicle on the other side of the bushes that ran along the perimeter of the property.

He put the truck in park, left the driver's door open, turned off the dome light, and grabbed one of the syringes from the cooler. Like lightning, Jason stealthily jumped from the cab just in time to see Andrea Harder open the rear door of the security building and lead Millie out into the darkness on her leash.

Jason froze in his place, the syringe gripped in his hand like a knife ready to stab. He watched her, listened to her, as she cooed at her pet. Millie did her business, then continued to sniff around. Andrea was patient with the animal, following it around willingly, until at last, Millie chose a spot and crouched to do the last of her business. It was then, at that exact moment, that everything in the universe lined up just right…

Andrea put her head back and looked up at the sky for the thousandth time that night. She inhaled deeply and closed her eyes. Jason stepped out silently, took two steps, and just as the dog turned in his direction, he grabbed her mistress and stabbed the needle into her neck, driving the plunger home.

"Ouch! What the…"

Andrea spun in his direction, the syringe still hanging from her neck. Millie, who Jason expected to bark, simply looked up at them both in the darkness, and Jason could see the dog's tail wag; she remembered him! When he turned his attention back to Andrea, she was just pulling the syringe from her neck; she looked down at it, her mind not registering exactly what she was seeing.

Even in the dark shadows of the yard, Jason could see her eyes as they began to glass over, and the reality of what he had done sent chills down his spine. What was he doing? Was he really going to abduct some girl who he really didn't know and keep her caged up in his basement? Was he going to do the same thing to her that had been done to him over in Afghanistan?

Andrea offered him a single confused look, then crumpled towards the ground.

Jason didn't think twice; he rushed forward and caught Andrea into his arms, putting her over his shoulder like a huge sack of laundry. Millie's leash slipped from her lifeless hand, but he didn't worry about grabbing it. Jason was relieved when he realized the dog was following him at his heels, that he wouldn't have to. He put Andrea behind the seat in the cab, straightening her out as best as he could on the bed he had made, and closed the half-door that gave access to that area.

"Are you ready to come to your new home, Millie-Mill?"

Bending down, he picked up the little dog, accepted a couple of licks to the face with a smile, then put her in the front, climbing in behind her. He activated the child-protection-lock so Andrea wouldn't be able to jump out and hurt herself if she woke, but he knew she wouldn't; Jason had given her plenty, enough to keep her subdued until well after he got back to Chesterfield, but it was always better to be safe than sorry.

"Here, Millie," he said as he pulled a snack out of his cooler and gave it to the pooch. "Let's take a ride, okay girl?"

CHAPTER 13

Andrea Harder was cold; she groped in the darkness for her blanket, but her senses were off. It was almost as if she were actually in a dream that she couldn't pull out off. She was sluggish, couldn't see, and her hands and arms felt as if they weighed a ton each.

She was thirsty, and as she struggled to regain consciousness, Andrea could feel that her head was throbbing. Her eyelids fluttered once, then twice, and she was then able to open them into a slit. The room was pretty dark, except for a small lamp lit in the next room. She could hear violins… so many violins, playing some kind of soft melody in the distance.

Where was she?

"Millie?"

No yips or barks came in response. Andrea was trying to sit up now, and her eyes were open a bit more. This was not her bed… this wasn't even her room, or apartment, for that matter! As her awareness sharpened, she began to make out the bars…

Andrea had awakened to find herself in some kind of jail cell.

Now, Andrea sat on the edge of the bed, her entire

body trembling. She wrapped both of her arms around herself to warm up, and as she did, Andrea began to look more closely at her surroundings.

She was sitting on a bed, but it wasn't just any bed; Andrea sat on a full-sized canopy bed, with a white lace canopy. There were two overstuffed pillows at the head of the bed which sported matching white lace shams; an antique oak nightstand with claw feet was next to her. She noted almost immediately on top was a plastic pitcher and plastic tumbler. Instantly, all other thoughts of checking out where she was disappeared; her terrible thirst drove her to investigate the pitcher more closely.

With shaking hands, Andrea reached out and grasped the pitcher; it was full! Slowly, she pulled it up and toward herself, then lowered her face over the open top. There was no smell; it had to be water! She put her lips on the rim of the pitcher and began to drink. Andrea gulped the cold, wonderful liquid until it sharpened the pain in her head and began to upset her stomach, then she carefully returned it to its place on the nightstand.

Now, it seemed, things were becoming clearer. She saw a large bookcase next to the nightstand; it was filled with books, the titles of which she could not make out in the darkness. On another wall was a large dresser with what appeared to be several stuffed animals on it. Then came the bars.

The bars took up space which seemed to be at one time a doorway between the room she was in and the one with the lit lamp. About one-third of the bars, in the middle section, made up what seemed to be a door; it had a massive padlock on it. At the base of the door was a slit about six-inches tall and eighteen-inches long; she mentally waved its existence out of her mind and began to walk to the bars.

Andrea grabbed two of the bars in her hands. They were ice cold to the touch. Squinting up in the darkness, Andrea could see that they had been installed into the ceiling and floor; the bars weren't going anywhere. That didn't stop her from trying to shake them and test them for weakness. It didn't take her long to realize that it was a pointless attempt.

"Hello? Hello! Is anybody there?"

She froze and listened as closely as she could, but other than the classical music pumping softly all around her, there was no sound. It almost seemed to Andrea that her voice was hitting nothing; there was no echo of any kind. She could feel panic welling up inside of her, so rather than just yell again, Andrea decided to scream.

"Help!!"

Suddenly, the volume of the music dropped.

Now she was holding her breath; had the music gone down? She didn't have to wait long to find out; in a few seconds, Andrea heard the sound of a door opening, then closing shut. The sound of the door was followed by the sound of footsteps coming downstairs.

Andrea strained her eyes in the darkness, trying to see anything at all. After a few seconds, the lights started to brighten slowly. Another couple of steps and the man turned the corner and came into view.

It was the guy from the park, the guy Brad beat up outside of the Watering Hole!

"Hello, Andrea," he said, a gentle, sweet smile on his face. "I have been waiting for you to wake up. As usual, you're right on time, just like with everything."

She was so shocked, and in such a state of dismay, that Andrea couldn't say anything at all in response. It was all she could do to stand there and try to process the situation she suddenly found herself in. Her mouth was wide open as her mind spun around the fact that the man from the park was standing on the other side of jail bars from her. He had brought her here on purpose, and the potential reasons for his actions were all rushing into her head at an alarming rate.

"Don't hurt me."

This was all she could muster. The thought of adding the word 'please' to the request didn't enter her mind at all. Andrea was scared, after all, she was aware of the grimness of the situation she was in. She had been kidnapped, taken hostage, for who knows what reason. In her mind, rape and murder were clear motives.

On the other side of the bars, in the room with the lamp, there was also a reclining chair, an end table, and a long bar with several items on top that Andrea hadn't yet registered. Her eyes stayed fastened on the man as he plopped down in the recliner, then pulled the lever to extend the footrest; his eyes held hers the entire time.

"Don't hurt you," he echoed calmly as he got comfortable. A slight smile came over his face. "You're concerned with me hurting you... isn't that comical, Andrea? Don't you think?"

His calm voice and demeanor were unnerving to her. The man reached up and began to stroke what appeared to be a fading bruise on his cheek. He stroked the bruise with his forefinger, up and down, over and over again, while he waited to see if she was going to give him some kind of response.

After a moment of nothing but silence from her, he put down the footrest and leaned forward. "Well, I guess you aren't ready to talk right now."

Standing up, the man walked around the long bar and inserted a key into a metal box fastened to the wall. Opening it, he removed an aspirin bottle, popped it open, and removed a single white pill. As he replaced the bottle and locked the cabinet back up, Andrea began to look furiously around the room, taking in as much of her surroundings as she could. When he turned back to her, she quickly focused her attention on him.

"I happen to know for a fact, that you probably have a pretty nasty headache." The man reached the bars and held out the pill. "Here is an aspirin. Don't worry, if I intended to kill or harm you, the job would be done and over—don't you think?" He gave her a wink that made her anger grow. Andrea glared at him and made no effort to take the pill from his open hand.

He glanced around her. "You found the water, I presume?" Andrea didn't reply. "Well, I'll just put this here, just in case you decide you need some relief." He balanced the pill on the central crossbar, then turned and walked back to his chair. "Do you remember me, Andrea?"

Andrea reduced her eyes to slits and gave two short nods. She was getting angrier by the second, and Jason knew it. Well, he had known there would be an adjustment period; he also knew there might never come a time he could let her out and begin to trust her. So, they had to start with baby steps.

"I don't know if you remember, but my name is Jason," he said, lacing his fingers together on his thighs, his feet reclined once again. "I met you in the park when you were walking Millie, remember that? I also tried to help you when your dolt of a boyfriend hit you, and you got my rear end beat. Oh, yes! Let's not forget how you embarrassed me, and yourself, by freaking out on me at the Cozy Cowboy, when all I wanted to do was bring you flowers."

"Nobody likes a stalker, mister," she told him through clenched teeth.

He gave her a disgusted snort. "I told you my name is Jason. So, I can tell by your attitude that it's time we have our little talk."

He stood up and began to pace, his hands clasped behind his back as he walked. Andrea simply watched him with her eyes, not moving another muscle in her body. She was so pissed! How dare this weirdo even think he could do something like this? Throughout her life, she had known men who thought they could hurt her, use her, and abuse her, but this was an all-time new low. Andrea decided, right away, that the first chance she got, she would cave in his skull.

"Who do you think you are?" she hissed.

Jason stopped and turned to her, a half-smile on his face. "I told you, Jason Brandtley. I told you that at the park, I told you that a minute ago, and I'm telling you now; why don't you learn to listen instead of shutting everything out in life that you don't like?"

He studied her for a moment, then continued. "Like I said, it's time for our talk. So, I know you are wondering why you're here; I guess I can fill you in. You're rude, but it isn't just that; you're also harsh, abrasive, and inconsiderate. The very attitude that you demonstrate to complete strangers, without even knowing who they are or what they are made of, is reprehensible. Do you enjoy being that kind of person?"

Jason held her stare, waiting patiently for an answer. Several minutes passed, and the pair continued to look each other in the eye, but finally, Jason gave a disgusted chuckle. He turned his back to her, walked away, and sat back down in his recliner.

"Well, what did I expect from such an obnoxious woman, other than more rudeness?" He flipped the lever again, and the footrest popped up, so he got comfortable. "Okay, fine. See this place?"

Andrea broke her stare and glanced around. As far as 'prisons' went, it was nice. The floors were carpeted, and the furniture in both rooms appeared to be new, or close to it. The artwork and electronics were also high-end, including the large flat-screen that hung facing her cell. She shifted her gaze back to Jason but held her tongue.

"Anyway, of course, you do; you see this place just fine," he continued. "Well, this is your home now, at least for the time being."

She cleared her throat gently; her mouth was still so dry, but taking a drink was the furthest thing from her mind. "What do you want? What are you going to do to me?"

Jason's smile softened. "Oh, I see; you think I'm going to hurt you or something. No, no, Andrea; you are in no danger of harm. But you are here for a very specific reason."

"And what would that be?" she whispered.

He clucked his tongue and shook his head. "You really don't know?" Andrea shook her head. "You're here to learn to be a decent human being to those around you. I can't think of anything that could have possibly happened to you in your life that would make you think you can be such a jerk to others."

Jason looked proudly around the room, then waved his arm. "I'd say you're in the perfect place to do that, wouldn't you?"

Tears were welling up in her eyes, making her angry at herself for showing weakness. "You're trying to tell me I need to change? What could have happened to you to make you lock somebody in a cage, you sick, demented freak?"

In a flash, Jason stood up, and in less than two long strides, he was standing in front of her. His eyes were hard and cold, like the bars, and Andrea felt a rush of fear. In a frightening whisper, he replied, "See? Careful how you treat people, Andrea. You never know who you're really messing with, do you?"

This guy was crazy! She wanted to look away, to run back to the bed, throw the covers over her head, and hide. Instead, Andrea decided to stare him down, just as she had been doing, and just as he was doing to her now. A single tear ran down her cheek, but she didn't bother to wipe it away.

"There are rules," he said as he began pacing again. "Just like in life, there are rules, and you need to know them if you ever want to walk out of here. First, understand that you are here to make a change: a change in your attitude, and therefore, your life. Until you learn to be kind, appreciative and show a bit more of a gentle spirit, you will reside in this room."

Her mind was racing, trying to figure out what she could do to take back control of the situation, but Jason seemed to know each and every thought in her head.

"You can scream all you want; I invested a lot of money in soundproofing your living space." He waved his arm again proudly. "Can't hear a thing from upstairs or outside; oh, yes, you are in my basement, by the way."

"How did you hear me, then?"

Jason patiently crossed the room and tapped on a white box with a couple of black buttons on it. "Intercom system; I control it from upstairs. I actually have had it on, waiting for you to wake, but I flipped it off when I came down. Now that you're up and about,

I'll leave it on whenever I am not with you if I'm home. Otherwise, it will be off at all times. Needless to say, it will be completely pointless to hurt your throat by screaming your head off, so save your breath."

Andrea continued to stare at him and listen to his words, frustration building up inside of her. Jason paid no mind to her behavior, though.

"So," he continued, "as you might have guessed already, there are rules. The longer it takes you to obey them and make the changes you need to make, the longer it will take you to get out of here and get back to your life. You are not here for me or my pleasure, contrary to any sick ideas you might have in your head. So, here goes… and listen closely.

"The first rule: you will be polite. You will use words like 'please' and 'thank you.' I know, I know, they sound foreign and unfamiliar to you, don't they? Well, figure them out."

He walked over to the bar and bent down behind it; Andrea heard the sound of a carbonated beverage being opened. When he straightened back up, he took a long slug off a cold soda. Jason held it out in an offering, but she ignored him. He took another, smiled, and shook his head.

"This brings us to the second rule: if you are spoken to, you will respond politely. Even if you don't have a direct answer to a question. For instance, 'No, thank you; no soda for me.' " He took another, much longer drink, then took his drink to the recliner and sat back down.

"You have clothes and books in your cell," he continued. "That is all you'll have for now. As you earn trust, I will give you some paper and something to write with, but for now, you have everything you could want or need. I will feed you anytime you are hungry. Fortunately for you, I work from home, so I'll be here all the time for you."

Andrea's head gave a blare of pain, causing her to squint; her hand automatically went to her temple, and Jason watched her, taking in her every movement.

"Don't forget that you have that aspirin there," he offered sympathetically, then he continued. "There will be no snide or nasty attitudes. No name calling, and no violence. These things will not be tolerated, and they will set you back from obtaining your goal of release.

"Next: classical music will play nearly all the time." Jason drained his drink and set the can on the end table before turning his gaze back to her. "Once you begin to calm down and get into the right state of mind, I will allow television. Until then, it is important to remember how therapeutic music is: it soothes the savage beast. My doctor taught me this after... after... never mind. Classical music it is."

"Are you kidding me?" Andrea asked sarcastically; she had always liked rock and roll.

Jason ignored her rudeness. "Don't worry, I'll be sure to turn it up high when I go back upstairs. Onward. I have Millie. She is upstairs, sleeping soundly on an overstuffed dog bed I bought for her. She is healthy, happy, and unharmed."

"My Millie?"

He flashed her an award-winning smile. "Yes! I knew you would be glad to hear that! When you show signs of getting better, I will bring her down to be with you. Until then, Millie stays upstairs with me. Don't worry," he told her, holding up a hand at her sudden anxiety, "I would never hurt her. Like I said, I'm not even going to hurt you, though a good spanking is really what you need."

Andrea's head was really pounding, even through her anger. She gave a sideways glance at the pill on the crossbar, then shifted her eyes back to him. How she needed something, but she was sure he was trying to poison her or drug her so he could take advantage.

"Go ahead and take it," he said, as though he was reading her mind. "It's just aspirin, it will reduce the headache."

With a shaking hand, Andrea slowly reached out and took the pill from the crossbar. She then backed up, toward the nightstand, keeping her eyes on Jason, so she could get a drink. After she had taken the pill, she sat on the edge of the bed and looked at him.

"You'll never get away with this," she said in a low, steady voice. "Someone will look for me. My boss, my boyfriend, someone."

Jason put down the footrest and leaned forward, his elbows on his knees. "Yes, Dana might. But otherwise, we both know you have no one, now don't we?"

She stood up and rushed to the bars, then spat at him, a large glob that she had worked up after taking the water. Jason smiled and stared at the spit on the carpet for a moment, then grabbed a folded towel from the bar and cleaned it up. He smiled the entire time he did it.

"Now, this is exactly the behavior I'm talking about, Andrea." He finished and tossed the towel into a laundry basket just outside her cage. "This is what you need to change. I'll tell you what; I'm going to give you some time to think. If you get hungry, or if you need anything that I haven't already thought of, just holler. I'll be sure to have the intercom on so I can hear you."

As he walked away, rounding the corner and out of sight, as she heard his feet on the stairs, she screamed. "The hell with you! I am my own boss; I do what I want, asshole!"

Jason didn't answer. The music suddenly got louder, and Andrea ran to the canopy bed and collapsed on it. She sobbed and screamed for the next twenty minutes, eventually crying herself to sleep.

CHAPTER 14

Jason closed the basement door behind him, flipped the newly-installed deadbolt, and leaned back against the door. He had been nervous about talking to her and now felt relief. Andrea Harder was much less intimidating when she was behind bars. He was sure now that this was the best thing for her.

After breathing for a moment, Jason righted himself and glanced over at Millie. The little Yorkie was sitting on her brand-new bed, ears perked up, studying him intensely. She must have heard her mom's screams when he came through the door.

"Mommy's okay, Millie," he said soothingly. The pooch's tail began to thump against the cushion, and she laid her head back down. "She'll be even better soon, puppy. Soon, she'll be like new."

Jason reached to the right and flipped a small switch on the intercom; nothing was coming from the basement but the sound of music. Satisfied, he walked away and began to hum the sonnet that was playing. It was so funny to him how his stress melted away when the music was on. It should be required listening for everyone.

A glance at the clock told him that it was time to check on Winnie and Rayne. There was supposed to be a storm that evening, and he wanted to make sure that Winnie's pain wasn't out of control. He pulled on his work boots, topped his head off with his Stetson, and went out the front door.

Kirk Hampton was just getting into his truck.

"How're all them sheep?" Jason hollered.

Kirk paused, looked at him, and smiled. "Really good; got some shearing to do tomorrow for the textile order, but otherwise, they're top-notch, Mr. Brandtley."

Jason had told the man several times to call him by his first name, but it never seemed to take. "Great," he replied. "Sure appreciate your hard work."

A strange look crossed Kirk's face. "I think your old mare might be having some problems. She's quiet now, but on my way to the pasture, I heard her moaning a bit."

"Yep," Jason said with a nod. "I'm gonna be putting her down in a few more days. I have an appointment with Doc Gale coming up. Maybe I'll have to move it up, though."

Satisfied, Kirk jumped in his truck with a wave and made his way down the gravel road and out of sight. Jason went to the office, where he filled two syringes. As he went back out to the stables, he was really more concerned right now with having enough injectable drugs to subdue Winnie. He made a mental note to go to Doc Gale for a couple more vials before the appointment for euthanasia.

Kirk was right; Winnie was a mess. She was lying down again, snorting and shaking her head back and forth in pain. Jason administered the first shot, waited, then gave her a second. Once she was calmed down, he checked their feed, spent some time with Rayne, and then headed back into the house. He suspected that Andrea had fallen back to sleep; now would be a good time to make her something to eat; soon she will wake up hungry.

He opened the door to the house and was greeted by Millie and her wagging tail. As Jason picked up the little dog and gave her some affection, he heard a drawer slam shut over the intercom. It had been an hour or so since he had left Andrea; it sounded like she was awake and going through the dresser.

Good, he would make her some lunch.

∞

Andrea had slept for a short time before waking up once again, her dry mouth tormenting her.

She had immediately remembered where she was this time, and as she sat on the edge of the bed drinking water, she had fumed. This crazy menace was really off his rocker. That was okay, though. He said he wasn't going to hurt her, and for some reason, she believed him. That didn't matter, though. She was going to find a way out.

Andrea had finished her water and began to look around the room. She took it slowly because she was still groggy, but she forced herself to get up and investigate her surroundings a bit better. He had to have missed something; there had to be some spot or area that he had failed to secure properly.

First, she had checked the bars again; the guy had really spared no expense, and the bars were not going to be her way out. Next, she went through everything, each dresser drawer included. He had bought her all brand-new clothes; they were expensive and stylish. In a way, Andrea found herself feeling bad for how she had treated him, but then she remembered that he kidnapped her, and she pushed her sympathy out of her mind.

Next, she found the bathroom, which had been hidden from view by a white lace curtain. It was spotlessly clean, and Jason had provided her with everything from shampoo to body wash, to the very best toothpaste. Unfortunately, her toothbrush was only about two inches long; Jason had removed the handle. Good thinking, she thought. I would've stabbed him with it if I could.

There were no cords of any kind, lighting was set into the ceiling; she couldn't even reach the fixtures when she stood on her bed or nightstand. It frustrated her to death that he had covered all his bases.

After about a half-hour of searching and seeking, she sat on the edge of the bed looking around her hopelessly. For now, anyway, she could find no resources to use that would help her. That was okay; Dana would miss her as soon as she didn't show up. The woman would drive to her apartment and, when she found no one home, would call the police. They would be looking for her soon enough; she just needed to bide her time.

As she sat on the bed, thinking and scheming, she noticed she could smell herself. Andrea glanced back at the curtain covering the bathroom area longingly. How good would it feel to let the hot water run over her skin? She could just imagine. But what if he came down while she was naked, and it spurred him onto violent behavior, like rape?

No, she didn't think he would do something like that. If he were at all concerned with raping or torturing her, Andrea would have noticed cameras around, or he would have skipped hanging the curtain altogether. He had actually thought about her and protected her modesty; Jason, in some sick, twisted sicko way, had thought about protecting her from shame or embarrassment.

Andrea got up, went to the dresser, and chose a pair of jeans, large hoodie, and undergarments. She then went into the bathroom area, where a built-in shelf was loaded with towels and washcloths. Soon, she was in the shower, scrubbing and enjoying the feel of it on her skin.

∞

Fifteen minutes later she pulled back the curtain, her arms laden with dirty clothing. She made her way to the bars so she could put the dirty items in the basket on the other side. Jason was sitting in his recliner, his eyes closed, enjoying the classical music. Andrea just stopped, frozen, and stared at him; almost immediately, he opened his eyes and smiled.

"Do you feel better?" he asked.

Noting that the music was low enough to talk, she nodded once, then approached the bars and began to slide the clothing through one item at a time. First, her work uniform; next, the towel and her dirty undergarments. When she was finished, she stepped back and sat down on her bed and looked at him.

"You can't change someone just because you think they need to change, you know," she said sternly.

Jason ignored her statement. "Are you hungry?" He stood up and took a plate of food and plastic tumbler from the bar. "I made you a sandwich: turkey and swiss with mayo, my personal favorite. I hope you like it too. There are some potato chips, as well, and this…" He held up the tumbler. "Is milk."

Andrea's mouth began to water immediately. She loved turkey and swiss with mayo; how long had this guy been following her around, anyway? It frightened her to think about it, but she was so hungry now that she was beyond caring. She nodded gently, her face softening and her stomach growling.

Jason brought the plate and knelt down to slide it through the narrow opening at the bottom. He then stood back up and held out the tumbler. He made it a point to smile kindly at her; she needed to eat, so now was not the time to be the strict disciplinarian.

"You'll have to come to get the milk," he said sheepishly. "It won't fit through the slot."

Slowly, she made her way to the bars. Ignoring the

food, she reached out and took the milk, her fingers brushing against his as she did so. Andrea almost cringed from the feel of his skin, but she fought the urge. Taking a step back, milk in hand, she bent down and picked up the plate of food; it looked incredibly delicious.

"I should warn you," Jason mentioned pleasantly as she sat on the bed, "I thought I would have lunch with you, is that okay?"

She didn't answer; instead, she took a huge bite of the deli sandwich and began to chew. It was amazing! When she opened her eyes after relishing in the pleasure of the meal, Jason was back in his recliner, a plate of food on his lap, and a cold glass on the end table beside him. They ate together in silence for a while.

About half-way through her meal, Andrea's stomach began to feel queasy. Putting the plate on the bed beside her, she began to slowly drink the milk, watching him over the rim of the tumbler the entire time. Finally, she put down the drink and looked up at him; he was focused entirely on the sandwich.

"I'm going to see to it that you are put away forever," she said with a hiss.

Jason didn't skip a beat, he simply nodded and chewed the bite in his mouth. After swallowing, he said to her, "Let me tell you a story, Andrea."

He put his plate on the stand next to his drink and turned his full attention to her. "I went to Afghanistan a short while back, to be a medic in the war. My mother hated the thought; since my dad had died, she was petrified that I would end up dead—terrified she would be all alone. Well, I wasn't there very long when I was taken prisoner. They put me in a small metal box, and there were no bars; I didn't know day from night, much like you. They put cigarettes out on me, beat me, and kicked the box around with me inside; those things are just the tip of the torture iceberg, though. My point? You probably will put me away for life, but nothing they can do to me will ever compare to what I've already been through."

Andrea stared at him, mouth open. This guy was really out of his mind! He had gone to war and snapped, and now she was going to suffer as a result. What could she even really make out of the situation she was in? She had heard about guys like him, and the situations they were in with other people after they had lost their minds were never good.

She looked down at her sandwich and thought for a minute. "What are you going to do with me?"

Jason looked at her, confused for a moment. "Like I said, I'm going to help you; didn't you listen to anything I said?"

"Of course, I did, dirtbag!" she shot back. "It just seems ridiculous that a man would abduct someone just to teach them to be a little nicer. I mean, rape and murder I can buy, but etiquette class? Come on!"

She was starting to get a little sassy; obviously, the food was bringing back her chipper spirit. Jason smiled at her, sat back, and focused on his food. The last thing he should do is feed into her negativity by validating her crap with a response.

Andrea stared at him; how could the jerk be so crude? She took a small bite of her sandwich, her mind turning things over and over. The police had to be looking for her by now; Dana had to be wondering where she was. It was true that she had no idea how much time had passed, or how long she had been down here, but it was certainly time for her to be at work, wasn't it?

"Is it Wednesday?" she asked after swallowing her tiny bite.

Jason nodded and took a long drink, then another bite.

"My boss…"

"I told you I wasn't going to hurt you," Jason said, a little irritated now. "I also told you that you aren't leaving here until you change your attitude. If they, for some reason, track you to me, then so be it, at least I tried. But if they don't, well, I'd get to work if I were you."

Her head was still swimming a bit. He was right; what were the chances of them tracking her here? Police would roust Brad Nagle before they even begin to recall the guy with the cowboy hat who brought flowers to her at the café; as a matter of fact, Dana had likely forgotten his existence. She knew that the chances of them finding her here anytime soon were slim.

Andrea put her plate on the bed and looked up at him timidly. "How is Millie?"

Now Jason looked up at her and smiled. "Millie is

great. She has yummy treats and a comfy bed, and I'm pretty sure she knows you're here. If you start making strides, I'll bring her down here to be with you."

A smile played at the corner of her lips as she thought about her little Yorkie. Millie had been her best true friend ever since she had her; she could feel nothing but relief that he hadn't harmed her little baby. He saw her smile, and it made him feel good.

"How long have you had Millie?" he asked.

Andrea's smile grew. "I got her when I moved into that apartment, about a year-and-a-half ago. She's the best; thanks for bringing her."

Jason studied her briefly. "See?" he asked after a moment. "Was it so hard to just be nice?"

Andrea didn't respond.

"You know," he continued, "If you had simply sat down in that booth the day I brought you the flowers and told me where you stood instead of flipping out and embarrassing me, this would not be happening. I would have walked away then."

She simply listened to his words, turning them over in the head as he kept on. "I would have gotten the clear picture, and so I would never have thought, 'she's just having a bad day; I'll try again later.' Which, by the way, is what I did the day that dirtbag hit you in front of that bar, the day I got jumped for trying to be a gentleman."

Deep in her heart, Andrea knew he was right. "You just caught me at a bad time in the café. I had a lot going on."

He waited.

"I don't really want to talk about my personal life," she mumbled.

Jason stood up with his plate and put the glass on the bar. "You don't have to, not unless you want to. Or, if you think it can help. I will always listen, and I don't want anything in return. This whole thing?" He waved the plate around the room, causing breadcrumbs to fall to the floor. "This isn't about me or what I can get; it's about you getting a little peace and tranquility so you can make better choices in men. You can't get a good man unless you are a good woman, and that involves more than finances and independence."

With that, Jason left the basement.

Andrea stared after him, not even noting that the music, once again, got louder. Her sandwich and chips sat forgotten next to her as his words echoed, over and over, through her head. It was as though she was just about to grasp some foreign truth but simply couldn't wrap her fingers around it. Wasn't she a good woman? She worked, lived on her own, and depended on no one; wasn't that what a good woman did? It was certainly more than her own mother ever did!

Placing the plate on the nightstand, Andrea lay back on the bed and continued to go over the things he had said to her. Thoughts of escaping had left her mind; she was too busy weighing words. She was a good woman, wasn't she? Wasn't that the reason all the men in her life had taken advantage of her?

Eventually, Andrea fell back to sleep. A better sleep

this time, one that wasn't worried about rape or murder. Asleep filled with the face of a man in a cowboy hat telling her she could be a better woman.

CHAPTER 15

Dana Grulkey stepped through the swinging kitchen doors of the Cozy Cowboy, a perfunctory smile on her face, and looked over the busy restaurant dining room. It was pretty full for a Wednesday, even during the lunch rush. She scanned the area, her eyes settling on each server present so she could make sure all hands were on deck for the rush.

With each person her eyes landed on, a name came to mind, and then she moved on to the next. Someone was missing! She began to look again, counting and thinking, counting and thinking. Suddenly, she knew! Where was Andrea?

One of the servers came rushing by with an empty water pitcher, her mind totally on her work. Dana reached out and touched the girl's arm to stop her. "Andrea's here, isn't she?"

With exasperation, she shook her head. "No, and Renee and I are having to pick up her tables. Could you call her?"

"Absolutely." Dana turned and went to the back of the house, toward her office. She felt agitated; Andrea was never a late-comer or no-show, so why would she choose today to oversleep?

She got to her office and grabbed her cell from the desk, looked up Andrea's number in her contacts, and punched Call. The phone went right to voicemail, causing her to knit her brow. That was a new one for her favorite employee; now she was turning off her phone to avoid coming in? That was something only the newcomers and fly-by-nights did.

"Andrea, it's Dana," she said into the phone. "You're late. As soon as you get this, you need to let me know and get your butt in here!"

She hung up just as another server came into her office with panic on her face. "We just got a ten-top, and they are in Andrea's section, Dana. We need help out here."

Dana tossed her phone back on the desk and rushed out to tend to the crisis at hand. Man, she was going to chew Andrea out good. She'd never had to do that before, which tugged at the back of her mind as she tied an apron around her waist on the run.

"Let's go do this thing," she told the girl. "I'm gonna put my foot in her butt when she gets here, trust me!"

∞

Andrea woke to the sound of footsteps on the stairs. As her eyes fluttered open and took in reality, she felt the feeling of dread. No, this wasn't some kind of bad dream, she was really in Cowboy Hat's basement, still. Didn't he understand that he was going to cost her a job? She began to feel extreme irritation, and she sat up gruffly.

"It's almost suppertime, Andrea," Jason's voice said as she focused her eyes. "In about fifteen minutes, anyway. If you want to get yourself woke up, I'll be down with the food in no time, okay?"

"I'm gonna get fired over this, you know?" Her voice was edged with contempt.

Jason chuckled. "Yeah, but at least you don't have to worry about getting killed."

He turned around and went back upstairs. The music was still playing low in the background; it seemed that the music was nothing more than one long requiem that never ended. It just kept playing, playing to her self-pity and anger.

She got up and used the bathroom, then ran a brush through her hair. It had still been wet when she fell asleep, and now it stood all over the place like she had been the victim of electric shock. After a short moment, she gave up and wet it down, then ran a brush through her hair once again.

It was chilly in her cage. Wrapping her arms around herself, she briefly considered wrapping up in her blanket for warmth. Then Andrea remembered the hoodie, so she found the garment, and gratefully pulled it over her head.

She was still angry, but she noticed that her anger had subsided somewhat. Even though the guy was obviously sick, he had made it clear that he had no interest in harming or abusing her. She still wanted to grab him by the throat and choke him to death for assuming it was okay to do this for whatever reason, but she was also starting to feel like maybe she would just choke him until he passed out. When he woke, she would give him a lecture of her own about kidnapping people.

Jason was coming down the stairs. She rushed over to the bed and sat down; the last thing she wanted was for him to think she was eagerly waiting for him, or anything. Andrea wanted to appear nonchalant like his little game wasn't affecting her in the slightest. It wasn't true, but that was what she wanted.

He came around the corner with a massive tray in his hands, walking gingerly to keep from spilling the items he was carrying. He set down the tray on the bar, then turned to her. There she sat, looking like she might be pulling herself together somewhat.

The smile on his face was bright, as were his eyes. For a brief moment, Andrea thought he was handsome; he had the brownest eyes and the most perfect teeth. Why did he have to be such a freak? Not to mention, why hadn't she noticed his boyish good looks before?

"I made grilled chicken, wild rice, and green beans; hope that's okay." Jason picked up her plate and tumbler and headed for the bars. Sliding her plate through, he said, "Since I can't give you silverware yet, I also brought you down some corn chips to scoop up the rice and beans with. Oh, and there are plenty of napkins."

Andrea rose and took the tumbler from his hand, then watched him return to the tray, where his own plate sat. She bent down, got her food, and then put her meal next to her bed before returning to grab the bag of chips he was offering her. Without a spoon or fork, she would definitely need them.

"What could I do with a real spoon, Jason?" she asked sarcastically.

He turned to her with a smile. "You do know my name! Awesome! To answer your question, you'd be surprised what a person can do with a spoon when they are in this kind of situation."

Chips in hand, she returned to the bed and sat down. The chips were in the shape of large scoops; they would work. This guy thought of everything, didn't he?

The chicken looked wonderful, perfect in fact. It had been grilled on a barbecue, and it was a juicy, succulent hindquarter. Andrea paid no real attention to the rice or beans; instead, she grabbed the skin on the chicken, tore it off, and stuffed it into her mouth in its entirety. The flavor was so incredible that she had to close her eyes while she chewed so she could savor it even more.

When she opened her eyes, she saw Jason staring at her, smiling. "You like it? It's my mother's recipe; she made the best-grilled chicken in three counties."

Andrea held her hand to her mouth to cover it as she responded. "It's amazing."

"Enjoy."

For the next fifteen minutes, they ate their meal, the beautiful music wafting around them. Even Andrea had to admit that the lulling melodies that came from the speakers were like velvet on her soul, and it made the food taste that much better.

"Do you drink, Andrea?" Jason suddenly asked.

By the time she focused her attention on him and wiped her mouth, he was finished with his food and waiting patiently and expectantly for an answer.

"Sure," she replied. "Sometimes I have a glass of wine… but drinking isn't something I can afford to do often."

Jason responded, "I will have a glass or two with dinner, but that's it; I really don't drink at all. Would you like some wine now?"

She didn't have to even think about it. Andrea had drained her tumbler of milk several minutes before, and she was still cleaning up her chicken bones and a few green bean stragglers. The sound of a glass of wine made her feel warm and fuzzy.

"Sure," she said shyly. "Please."

Jason stood, still smiling, and went behind the bar. "See? You know how to be kind and polite; someone taught you manners, didn't they? I'm sorry the wine is in a plastic cup; this is a Sauvignon Blanc."

Andrea stood up and approached the bars so she could take the wine from him. "Of course, someone taught me manners. I mean, I wasn't raised by apes. You know, Jason, sometimes when bad things happen to people, they simply act the way they do as a means of protecting themselves. I mean really, think about what you're doing here, with me."

She sat back down on her bed after taking a long sip.

"Mumm, a zesty fruit flavor, I like it." Andrea tipped the cup towards Jason, as she picked up her plate; he responded to her.

"Yes, I know what you mean. But there is a difference between operating out of self-preservation and just being ill-mannered." This time she didn't reply to his statement, she simply grabbed a new chip and pushed the remainder of her beans onto it with her finger. "So, with that being said, what happened to you that causes you to want to protect yourself?"

As she chewed, Andrea looked up at him and considered the fact that he was trying to casually, if not intensely, converse with her. Should she even play a part of any kind in his sick little fantasy game? She shrugged mentally; at this point, what would it hurt? After all, she would die of loneliness before she would die of starvation or exposure.

"I'm like anyone else." She took another sip, as she swirled and sniffed the cup to smell the aroma. "Bad things happen to everyone, mine just involve men who seem to think that the only thing a woman is for is a possession."

Jason took a sip of his wine as he thought about her response. "I can't say the same thing, even from the male perspective," he told her. "I mean, girls have never treated me like a possession; mostly they just treated me like a wad of dirt they discovered smashed into the tread of their shoe." He paused and took another drink. "You included."

She had been chewing her last bite when he said

this, and the sharpness of the statement made her stop mid-chew. Obviously, this guy had his heart broken a time or two. Andrea, in all her infinite wisdom, had managed to step on him once again without even really knowing why she was doing it, and she did that after he had been in the war. Boy, she was a bright one.

Placing the cup with all the plates, she carried them, with the tumblers, to the bars and slid the plates through the slot near the floor. Jason walked over to her, holding her gaze, and took the tumblers from her. He wasn't smiling now; he was studying her, wondering if she had paid any attention to his words at all.

"Thanks for thinking of the dishes; I like clean surroundings, and I had sort of spaced them off from lunch. I appreciate it." He turned around to place the items on the large tray on the bar.

"You know, I had no idea," she mumbled, embarrassed. "I was just having a bad day."

Jason spun around. "Which day? The time you screamed at me in public, or the time you almost got my head caved in?"

Andrea felt tears coming to her eyes. "Both, I guess."

He noticed that she was getting emotional, and Jason felt ashamed for being so uptight. He hadn't brought her here to abuse her, not physically, and certainly not emotionally or mentally. He was letting his own hurt feelings come in the way of the true purpose of all of this.

"I'm sorry," he said, looking into her eyes. "I guess

I'm still a little raw, but that's no excuse. I apologize."

Andrea nodded, brushed self-consciously at the tears, and walked back to her bed.

"My mother just died recently," he told her as he took his seat once again, glass in hand. "I don't remember if I told you that when we met in the park or not, but she did. Cancer. She was my biggest fan. If she knew I had gone to this extreme just to prove a point, she would have beat me like she was a man." He chuckled. "When you are kind, when your temper is under control, you remind me of her; you even have the same hair color and eyes. I think that might be why I was... I don't know... drawn to you, or something."

She listened to his words. "Were you close?"

"I was very close to both of my parents," he shared. "Well, being an only child, it's a bit unavoidable."

Andrea began to twiddle her thumbs, and she stared down at them as if they held the secrets of the universe. "I'm an only child too, but things didn't really go the same way for me."

"What happened?"

She looked up at him abruptly. He looked truly interested in what she had to say, hanging onto her every word. Andrea had never known a man that wanted to hear anything about her life, or about her as a person. They wanted her to stand at their side, look pretty, keep her mouth shut, give them her money, and pleasure them when the mood struck. She cringed inwardly at the honesty she was doling out to herself. Jason, on the other hand, was sitting forward in his recliner, waiting for her response like a kid who is next in line to ride the roller coaster.

"Why do you care?" she asked. "I mean, I'm not trying to be rude. It's just that, well, no one really ever cares about anyone else's life, do they? Isn't it all just a put on?"

A confused look came over his face. "I don't know, Andrea. All I can tell you is that I care; I'm interested. You know, my mother used to say that all of the experiences of one's life make up who they are. If I want to understand you and why you do the things you do, well, getting to know about your life is really the only way to accomplish that."

She leaned her back against the head of the bed and looked at him, thinking about the statement he had just made. It made a lot of sense; of course, we are a conglomeration of things. Whether we are rude or polite, funny or harsh, our experiences are the primary contributing factors.

"That makes sense," she said thoughtfully. "I guess I never really thought about it, but it would explain a lot about the ways people have treated me in my life."

Jason glanced up at the wall above the bars. "It's getting late. I have to tend to Winnie first thing in the morning; the night will be hard on her."

"Winnie?"

Jason nodded, a sad look in his eyes. "Winnie is our mare, or I should say, my mare. She's about as old as I am, but she is in a lot of pain… her hips are going bad. I made an appointment with her vet to come put her down, but that won't be for a couple more days. In the morning, I'll be going to Chesterfield to get her some pain medication. Please, don't try to yell or get anyone's attention. You'll just upset Millie, and no one will be able to hear you; we're here alone."

Andrea didn't respond. As soon as he told her that he would be going to town in the morning, she couldn't help but start plotting. If there were a way out, tomorrow morning would be a good time to find it. She believed him about the screaming, though. If he had gone to the financial lengths he had to build the cage, he wouldn't have left out soundproofing. No, the solution would lie in finding a way out.

"I hope you have a good night," he said. "Do you want me to leave the lights up for a bit so you can read? They're on a timer, so it's easy enough to do."

"Yes, please."

Jason seemed very happy with the use of the word 'please.' He smiled at her, then said, "It's going to be fine for you, Andrea. No matter what happens to me in the end, I am going to see to it that your time here is nothing less than beneficial to you as a person. That way, when you go on with your life, you will make some man very happy."

He turned and walked out of sight, his footsteps and the door upstairs closing the last signs of life she got from him for the night.

Andrea rose and walked over to the bookshelf. She chose a familiar horror novel about zombies taking over a cruise ship and took it back to her bed. Now that she knew he would be leaving in the morning, she couldn't stop thinking about escaping. Even as she read the book, her mind went over different options as far as where she could look, or what she could do, to get out of the house and away from Jason.

But as she dozed off, book in hand, he entered her thoughts, and her gentle captor invaded her dreams.

CHAPTER 16

"Renee, can I see you in my office for a second, please?"

Big Dana had been in a stern mood since about a half-hour after opening the restaurant, and it had sparked several whispers behind her back from her staff. She didn't care, though; she didn't open a restaurant to make friends. Right now, she was more concerned with the fact that her best server hadn't shown up to work for the second day in a row. Again, there had been no call.

Dana had left several messages on Andrea's cell phone, and after closing the night before, she had even driven past the girl's apartment building. Unfortunately, there had been no lights on at all in the building at that hour, so she had been forced to ring the apartment over and over for fifteen minutes, all to no avail.

It disturbed her that the last time she spoke to Andrea, the girl had refused a ride home. What if some killer had gotten his hands on her? Worse yet, what if that dirtball Brad had taken her somewhere and was beating on her, even as she thought about it? Andrea had no one in her life; that much she knew. Dana

Grulkey felt like she had an obligation to find the girl, or at least figure out whether or not she was okay.

"What's up, Dana?"

Renee Clovis stood in the door of her office, an expectant look on her face. The older woman was in her late fifties and had been waiting tables since the cook was a pup. Today, she looked terribly worn out, and why not? Dana and her staff had been covering tables for the missing Andrea for two days, and that was a major amount of work.

"Have you heard anything from Andrea at all?" she asked Renee.

Renee shook her head. "You know I don't socialize with these kids outside of this place."

Dana's stomach was in knots; something was wrong. "What about that character Brad, you know, the dirtbag she was dating?"

Renee knit her brow. "You know, come to think of it, I do happen to know that he hangs out at the Watering Hole. A few months back, I dropped her there after work because it was raining. She happened to mention that was his regular spot. You don't think…?"

Dana snatched up her cell to search for the number. "I don't know what to think. All I can say is that Andrea doesn't do this, and that guy was a psycho who she just happened to have recently dumped. Thanks, get back to the floor, please."

Dana found the number and pressed the call button. While it rang, she nervously tapped her pen on a stack of food acquisition forms on her desk. If she found out that Andrea had just been slacking off, she was fired. She hated to have to do it, but she had a business to run!

"The Hole, how can I help you?"

Dana sat forward in her chair and stopped the tapping. "Um, I'm looking for the boyfriend of a friend of mine to give him a message… she's sick. Brad is his name?"

"Brad Nagle?"

She was getting impatient. "Big guy; likes to act tough. My friend's name is Andrea."

"Brad! You got a call!"

Dana breathed a sigh of relief as the person on the other end put the phone down with a clunk. She could hear music and drunken laughter, and soon the phone was retrieved by the guy they called to the phone. Immediately, Dana knew she had the right dirtbag.

"It's Brad," he sneered. "Whadda you want?"

"Brad? This is Dana at the Cozy Cowboy; I'm calling about Andrea Harder."

Brad snorted. "I ain't seeing that chick no more."

She closed her eyes and tried to keep calm. "I know. I just didn't know who else to call. You see, Andrea hasn't been to work in two days; she hasn't called, and there's no answer at her place. I was hoping you knew where she was."

He paused, and for a moment she was concerned that he had hung up. "Brad?"

"Yeah, yeah," he replied. "She ain't been to work?"

"No, Brad. She has not."

"Wow."

He was stinking drunk, and likely having a difficult time putting her words together. "Look," she told him, "I didn't mean to bother you. I just wondered if you had talked to her."

"No, it's no problem," he replied, his voice suddenly much clearer. "I just... I can't believe she's missed work. She never does that."

Dana said nothing.

"Look," he continued, now sounding pretty sober. "Let me check around; maybe she's sick or something. There's an old couple in her building, but they won't talk to me. You might want to ask them; their names are Gravis or Gravitz. Yeah, that's it: Mr. and Mrs. Gravitz."

Dana noticed that his tone had taken on a bit of worry, and she knew he wasn't smart enough to fake it. "Thank you, and please let me know if you hear anything."

"You know, she is mad at me. I would say that maybe she went home to old North Dakota, but her and her mother don't get along." Once again, he paused. "Wow. I hope she's okay."

"So do I."

Dana hung up the phone and stood up grabbing her purse and car keys off the desk. She went through the kitchen, telling her cook staff that she was stepping out for a bit, then did the same with her servers in the dining room. Without waiting for a response of any kind, she climbed into her SUV and took off out of the

Cozy Cowboy parking lot and up the avenue towards Andrea's apartment.

∞

Andrea had her nightstand pulled out from its place. She was moving it around the cell looking high and low for any weak spots or windows of any kind. The nightstand was acting as a stool for her; she was glad that it was solid oak, but it sure was heavy.

She had been at it for hours, and so far, she had absolutely no luck whatsoever. Andrea was to the point that she knew he had done an outstanding job constructing this place. Jason had built it with full intentions of it being escape-proof, and from the looks of it, he had succeeded.

He had come down that morning with a breakfast of pancakes, eggs, bacon, and hashed browns, as well as milk and juice. It had been delicious, even though she couldn't shake the fear that she was going to get fat living there. Jason had eaten with her, talking about Winnie the horse, and making sure she didn't need any items from town. Since he had been so thorough, even providing her with her choice of feminine hygiene products, she could think of nothing she was lacking.

Andrea jumped down from the table and groaned. That was it; she had inspected pretty much every inch of the walls, ceilings, and floors. She moved the table back to its designated spot, then plopped down hard on the bed, tears of frustration welling up in her eyes. She wanted out! She was going to lose her job, her apartment, and all of her belongings! Didn't he care about that at all?

She began to wonder if she just gave in, kissed his rear and played the 'good girl,' how long it would take him to let her go? What would she do if that really happened? Andrea knew what she would do: she would run to the police so fast his head would spin, and she was sure he knew it. That's why she was convinced he would never let her go. Even if he never harmed her, he wouldn't let her go.

She thought about making a weapon of some kind, but there was nothing she could use. He had removed the handles off everything, from her toothbrush to her hairbrush. The only solution would be to gain his trust enough for him to give her eating utensils. Then she would have something to work with.

Andrea just stood up to blow her nose when she heard the music lower; Jason was back.

Hurrying, she blew her nose, splashed water on her face, and checked her reflection. Would he be able to tell she had been crying? Probably, but she hoped he didn't ask her about it. If he did, she would tell him she was missing Millie.

"Andrea?" His voice was close now, so she came out of the curtained bathroom area and forced a smile.

"Hi," she said softly. "That didn't take you long."

He smiled and held out a paper bag to her. "Nah, Chesterfield is close. I brought you a jelly donut. Hope you like them."

Andrea smiled, and her mouth began to water as she took the bag. "Thank you. Actually, they're my favorite." She didn't want to know if that was information he had gleaned from following her, but she hadn't had a jelly donut in months, so she doubted it.

"There are napkins in the bag," he added. "Well, I got the medicine I needed for Winnie, and I confirmed the date to put her down. Doc Gale will be out in a few days to do it."

Silently, Andrea swallowed a bite of the donut, which tasted like some kind of gourmet pastry. She couldn't imagine how Jason felt about Winnie.

"Well, when you truly love something or someone, you want what's best for them," he replied. "Even if it hurts you, or if you have to let them go. Winnie is like family, and she's at the end of her happy trail. It's abusive to keep her here longer."

She gave him a slight nod and then focused on demolishing her donut. Jason ran upstairs briefly, and when he returned, he had milk for her to wash it down with. She took it from him gratefully and drained the tumbler in less than a minute flat.

"Cold," she said. "Good."

Jason watched her with a grin. She was loosening up a bit. He sat down in his recliner, and that was when the smile faded. Andrea didn't notice right away; she was busy walking back to her bed.

"Andrea, did you move the nightstand?"

She jerked her head up, looked at him with alarm, then glanced at the stand. That was when she noticed the black mark of a grease pencil running vertically beside the stand, on the wall. Jason knew where that stand should sit, and it was not in its proper place. There was no sense in lying to him.

"Uh, yeah," she said, turning back to him. "Yes, I did."

"Why?"

She tried to think up a believable lie, but her heart was pounding so hard she couldn't think. Would this be the thing that set him off, that caused him to strike her or otherwise hurt her? Well, there was only one way to find out.

"I was standing on it," she said firmly, without flinching from his gaze. "I was looking for a way out."

Andrea got chills as his old relaxed smile came back immediately. "Honesty… is vital, and now you have a bit of my trust because of it. I knew you would look, and that's fine. But like I said, there is no way out. You would need power tools, dear, and I made sure those were all out of reach. So, do you want anything special for lunch?"

Amazingly, his question didn't perturb her at all. As a matter of fact, his words prior to it made her feel… good. She had a rush of emotion similar to that of pride. He trusted her, even if it was for a trivial reason. She had been honest, just like he was completely honest when he said she would find no way out.

Maybe it was time to just play his game and get this over with.

"You know," she began, "I really liked the turkey and swiss."

Jason jumped up, obviously pleased. "Great! You

aren't too full from the donut?"

"Well, maybe a little…"

"No sweat, we'll wait an hour; how does that sound?" After she gave him a nod, he continued. "How about we play a game of cards to pass the time. Do you like Rummy?"

Andrea didn't feel like playing cards, or any other games, for that matter. But if she were going to 'play his game,' well, she would probably have to play other games, too. Well, at least he didn't want to take advantage of her to pass the time.

"Sure."

Jason trotted back upstairs, so Andrea stood at the bars waiting for him. Something in her heart was off; how could she be so calm, and why did she care that she had earned a little of his trust? She didn't know; all she knew was that, for the first time since she woke up in the cell, she felt like some kind of progress had been made in the right direction.

Whatever that direction was…

CHAPTER 17

"Mr. Gravitz, my name is Dana Grulkey. I'm Andrea Harder's boss at the Cozy Cowboy. I was wondering if I could have a word with you and your wife, please?"

Dana stepped back from the intercom outside the main entrance of the building and waited for a response. She was tapping her foot rapidly but was unaware of it. At that moment, Dana felt more anxiety than she had felt in a very long time, even when it came to running the restaurant. The fact was, she had come to love Andrea like the daughter she never had, and she was on the verge of hysterics regarding the fact that she couldn't locate the girl.

"Sure, Ms. Grulkey," the old man's voice said. "I'll buzz you in. Just pull the door when you hear the sound."

Dana was flooded with relief at his cooperation. Maybe Andrea had been sick, and the Gravitzes had been caring for her and forgotten to call into her job. The old man sounded cheerful and unconcerned; Dana thought she would be able to clear this up soon.

She took hold of the doorknob just as it buzzed and gave it a hard jerk. It opened easily. The Gravitz apartment was listed as 2A. That would be easy enough to find.

The entryway was small, with a large silk plant in a corner to the right. To the left was a row of eight mailboxes. She looked at 2A and saw 'Gravitz,' then let her eyes go to 2B; the name 'Harder' was written on a tiny slip of paper in Andrea's flowing script. Dana's heart gave a twinge of affection, and she headed up the half-flight of stairs that went to the second floor.

The corridor on that floor was long, with doors on the left and on the right. The first on the left sported plastic letters: 2A. This was it. She pressed the small rectangular black button beneath the peephole, and a loud chime came from within the residence. In a fraction of a second, a chubby man in plaid golf shorts opened the door with a broad smile.

"Ms. Grulkey, I presume?"

Mr. Gravitz stepped back and held the door open for her, letting her pass by him. "Go ahead and have a seat in the living room."

She stepped into a quaintly-decorated space that was obviously inhabited by the elderly. An old woman sat in a rocker watching TV; as soon as she saw Dana, she turned off the set with the remote and gestured to the sofa. Dana smiled and sat down.

"This is my wife Lorna, and my name is Herb." The old man sat in a loveseat to Dana's right, which matched the sofa perfectly. "Did Andrea have an accident at work today?"

Dana's heart sank; they didn't know where she was,

or they would be aware she wasn't at work. "Um, no, Mr.- I mean, Herb. That's why I came. Andrea hasn't been to work in two days, and it's just not like her to not show or call. Her ex-boyfriend mentioned you might know where she is, which is why I'm here."

The smile fell from the old man's face right away, concern taking its place. "Why, no! I haven't seen nor heard from Andrea for… oh, my… since Tuesday night." He turned to his wife. "Have you, Dear."

Lorna Gravitz's brow was knit with concern, her forehead creased with worry. She simply shook her head, her expression that of someone trying to recall something very difficult. Dana turned back to Herb, clasping her hands in her lap so they wouldn't be able to see them tremble.

"She was okay then?" Dana asked.

Herb nodded. "It was late… after eleven at night, I think. I heard someone coming up, so I looked out the peephole and saw her heading to her apartment. She was wearing her work clothes, so I figured she was just getting home."

Dana nodded; that all sounded right. So, no one had seen her since, no one they knew of, anyway. Her heart was heavy with dread. What had happened to her? Dana was no longer mad at her employee; now she was on the verge of panic.

"You didn't see her the following day at all?" Dana leaned forward. "Not getting her mail, or with her dog, or anything? She didn't have to work yesterday until the lunch shift, but today she was scheduled this morning;

she didn't show up for either one."

Herb turned to his wife, alarm taking over his face, then turned back to Dana. "You say that Brad character told you to check with us?"

Dana nodded.

"Well, if anyone hurt her, it would be him." His voice was firm and convincing, tinged with anger. "That jerk! Forgive me, Dear." Lorna nodded her forgiveness. "I'm telling you, he was violent and mean; well, I had to point my gun at him to get rid of him before!"

She thought about that. Had she let his tone of voice fool her? Dana had met Brad before, more than once, and while he was a burly boy, she didn't think he was smart enough to be so convincing. She wasn't going to let the gun incident slide, though. She was going to track Brad down and talk to him herself.

"Do you happen to know where he works?" she asked. "When I spoke to him earlier, it was on the phone. I think I need to talk to him face to face."

Lorna spoke up for the first time, pointing an arthritic finger toward the window, as though the loser was standing right outside. "That boy wouldn't know a job if it bit him in the butt! I think he works here and there, but he was always borrowing money from Andrea and not paying her back. The best place to find him is at the bar up the road."

They were right; he was likely still sitting there, drinking. Even if he had done as he said and made a few calls, Dana was sure he had done it from the comfort of a barstool. Can't expect much more than that from men like him.

Dana stood up, a fake smile on her face that didn't match her emotions. "Well, I'm so sorry to bother you two. I'm going to drive up to that bar and try to talk to him again. Thank you for your time."

Herb stood as well and followed her to the door. "You make sure to let us know when you track her down. Andrea doesn't have anyone here, you know."

Dana stopped in the hall and nodded. "I know; that's what worries me the most about all of this."

∞

"Gin!"

Jason fanned his hand out and set it gingerly on the carpet outside Andrea's cell, making sure that she could see all of his melds clearly. The pair had gotten sick of Rummy after one game, but its cousin seemed to be just right for both of them.

"Oh, man!" Andrea threw her head back and closed her eyes. "I was so close! Look!"

She had one card to get rid of, and she was disgusted. He had beaten her both games so far now; she was ready to take him by storm in a third. She reached through the bars and grabbed his cards, then put them all together and started to shuffle.

"One more?" she asked. "I need retribution."

Jason smiled and shook his head. "Fine. You just don't know when to say you've had enough, lady! How about a glass of wine?"

Andrea nodded and began to deal. She couldn't believe she was having fun in this guy's basement, as his hostage, no less. The two of them had laughed more in the last few hours than she had in the last three years combined. It was difficult to hate someone when there was such a smooth rapport, even if he had kidnapped you.

Jason brought back wine, they drank together and then began to sort their hands. Andrea finished before him, excited. Looked like she might have a chance if she kept getting cards like these. She watched him, looking at his features, his hair, his eyes. He was really good-looking; she would die to have lashes like his.

"Why aren't you married, Jason?"

Jason's smile didn't falter at all; he simply shrugged and thought about what the right answer would be.

"I was never the 'ladies' man,' if you know what I mean. I had a couple of girlfriends, but…" he paused, his eyes taking on a far-away look. "But they both eventually discovered I was not what they wanted or needed. Then I joined the service and went overseas… the rest is history."

Andrea nodded and put a couple of cards in order in her hand. "Same story, different lead."

"Tell me, Andrea; how about you?"

Immediately, her face clouded over. Why did she go and ask a question like that? A question that would spark a big disclosure? She wanted to dodge him, but he hadn't dodged her, now had he?

"Well, I'd have liked to, but I guess I'm too picky."

Jason snorted softly. "Picky? Why? Because you don't want to be bound to someone who uses you and abuses you? Sounds pretty sane, to me."

She looked up at him and smiled. "Yeah. Maybe I'm not 'picky.' Maybe I'm not the wench they all say I am."

"Now," Jason remarked, "that's not to say that you can't be one! I've had firsthand experience!" He laughed for a bit. "I should point out that there is a time and a place; you just have a hard time identifying that."

Jason let the subject drop, and they started their game. They played through, with Andrea winning every hand, laughing and jesting the entire time. Jason felt as though if nothing else, they were going to be friends, and that made him feel good. She was starting to understand that he meant her no harm. That didn't mean she wasn't going to bust him out to the cops as soon as he released her, but he didn't care. He just wanted her to respect herself and others more; when that happened, the days of drunken brutes would be over for Andrea Harder.

It was early afternoon by the time they finished, and Jason left her to go make their supper: hamburgers and fries. She lay down with her book, intending to read while she waited, but Andrea found that even the book couldn't hold her attention. The fact was, in the short time that was their afternoon together, she had begun to see Jason Brandtley in a whole new light. What if he really had her best interest at heart? Were there really men out there like that, and if so, was he one of them? Had she misjudged him so terribly?

Yes, she was starting to think she had.

But the fact remained that she was more than

apprehensive about letting him get too close. Regardless of his lack of desire to harm her, she wasn't ready to form any friendships, even if they were innocent. Aside from Big Dana, she didn't even let her co-workers get close. Andrea Harder had a wall around her, that much she was painfully aware of.

She closed her eyes, comfortable and secure in the canopy bed. Maybe she would just forget about all of this worry and take a nice, peaceful nap. Jason would wake her up to eat, and she was so content that a nap would be a pleasure.

It was so nice, even in the situation she was in, to not have to worry about anything for the first time in her life.

CHAPTER 18

Jason closed the basement door gently behind him, then rested his palm against it, as though his touch was lingering on her skin. Resting his forehead against the door, he smiled. It seemed that things were moving along.

When he pulled away and went into the kitchen to prepare supper, he hummed to the music. He wondered if Andrea could cook, or if she had any hobbies she enjoyed. From what he could piece together, she did nothing but work. He had concluded a couple of weeks ago that she used her job to escape thoughts of her personal life. While he didn't know anything about her childhood, he did know that her adult life had been horrible. He would probably work like crazy, too.

Andrea was talking to him, really talking to him. They had interacted socially by playing cards and enjoying some wine. They had asked each other personal questions, and she had been honest in her responses, he believed. Lies tended to be flowery and fake; the truth was usually painful, and Andrea's eyes had been filled with pain and apprehension when she spoke. Yes, Jason believed she had been completely honest.

This wasn't to say he trusted her. No, it was still far too soon for that; it had been two days. For all he knew, she was a wonderful actress, putting on airs and pretenses, and telling him what she thought he wanted to hear. That was fine; he was prepared for that. What he wasn't prepared for was the honesty. In fact, it now seemed to Jason Brandtley that the entire reason for her attitude, distrust, and anger could be how others had treated her.

The same with him and his fears and personal pain.

But he was going to continue on. He knew that he was head over heels in love with Andrea. But he was also fully aware that she would likely never love him. That made no difference to Jason; by the time this was over, he would have made a permanent impact on her life for the better. Even if he wound up spending the rest of his life in prison, it would be worth it to know that he had set her free from the prison of her own heart.

While the burgers sizzled in the pan, he checked the deep fryer temperature; it was nearly time to do the fries. He had whipped up a salad before going into Chesterfield that morning: a spinach salad with olives, sunflower seeds, and a sprinkle of parmesan cheese. Jason remembered that he had failed to ask her what dressing she preferred, so he turned down the music and put his ear against the intercom; he could hear nothing from the basement.

"Andrea?"

Releasing the button, Jason listened again. All he could make out was faint snoring; Andrea was napping, and it made him smile. Well, he would take down several flavors, and she could choose any of them she liked.

In minutes, he was dropping French fries and thinking about their conversation. Yes, Andrea was in prison, both in her own head and in her heart. But what about him? What kind of hypocrite was he? He never thought about it during his waking hours, but he had nightmares of the box every night. If a car backfired, his adrenaline went into overdrive. If someone raised their voice, even for the smallest reason, he jumped clean off the ground. If he were totally honest, then he would have to admit that these things kept him in prison as well.

Jason had brought his metal box home with him, and he was still living in it. They were both in cages, in their hearts, and in their lives. His heart began to pound and tears came to his eyes; Jason ran over to the disc changer and turned up the volume once again. Like Andrea's work, the music drowned out his own self-realization.

Smiling, Jason wiped his eyes, then grabbed the spatula so he could flip his burgers.

∞

Dana slammed her car door shut hard and pressed the alarm on her key fob. She looked at the small dive across the street and shook her head. The Watering Hole was just that… a hole. It was precisely the kind of place she would expect a lowlife like Brad Nagle to hang out, just the sort of establishment that scum would take a woman to for a 'good time.' Why did Andrea always settle for less?

Squaring off her shoulders and taking a deep breath, Dana started for the bar. The street was dead, so she crossed right away, then was greeted at the door by two patrons exiting: a girl in a halter that was coming untied was being led out by a hairy-faced, cross-eyed drunk man who was trying to help her walk.

"S'cuse us…" the man slurred.

Dana stepped back and let them pass, holding the door as they went. She watched them start off on foot, glad they weren't trying to drive. What a life, she thought. Andrea could have so much better than this.

When the couple turned the corner out of sight, Dana entered the bar. Coming into the dim lighting from the bright outdoors caught her off guard, and Dana was forced to pause until her eyes adjusted. When they did, she could see a long bar to her left, going down the length of the establishment. A man with long greasy hair was washing glasses; he looked up, gave her a cheerless nod, and went back to his task. At the bar sat a girl in dirty blue jeans and a t-shirt with cut-off sleeves. She was steadying herself on a young man who looked like a lumberjack; he didn't look half as drunk as his sloppy conquest.

At the end of the bar, she could make out the Dudes and Dames restrooms, which sported a single pool table before them, complete with low-hanging light. Five round tables were lined up to her right, each tall, and each flanked with high-backed stools that had seen better days. At the far table were two men; one of them was Brad Nagle.

With a grim expression, Dana made her way to the table. She meant business; she wasn't here for a good time, and she wanted the guy to know it. How could he even be sitting here drinking when Dana had told him she couldn't find Andrea? True love was a pain, ha.

As she approached the table, the guy sitting with Brad looked in her direction, his eyes bloodshot. Brad took no note of her; he just kept rambling on and on, telling whatever pathetic story he was telling. Dana went directly to him and put her elbows on the table, leaning in.

"Brad, remember me? Andrea's boss, Dana?"

The man's head wobbled as it turned to her; he was inebriated. There was no way he was capable of functioning. Her eyes scanned over him as best as she could in the dim lighting; she saw no scratches or bruises on his arms or hands, and she could make out no blood on him, but his t-shirt was black.

"Hey! Hey, you! Dana, right?" She caught a huge whiff of his breath and jerked her head back. "Hey, did you find Andrea? I'm really worried about her…" His drunk face suddenly started to scrunch up; he was getting ready to cry!

"Did you do something with Andrea, Brad? Did you hurt her?" Dana's voice was getting high, and she was using a very authoritative tone with him. He just started shaking his head.

"No! Naw! I would never!" Snot was coming out of his nose. "Maybe we just weren't meant to be, but you don't kill a girl for that! You get drunk and get over it!"

Dana studied him. He seemed unaware of her presence now that he went back to his drink. Brad Nagle might have been a good for nothing loser, but she didn't believe that he hurt Andrea. He could barely hold his eyes open.

With a swift slap to his shoulder, she thanked him and walked away. The bartender held her eyes as she approached him; now he was drying glasses with a grimy towel, and he kept up his pace while they stared.

"I'm sorry to bother you on such a busy day," she greeted sarcastically. "You know Andrea, right? The girl that dated Big Daddy over there?"

Long-Hair nodded and kept staring. "Well, I'm her boss; she didn't show up for work; have you seen her?"

The guy smirked. "Wow, you're a hound dog of a boss, huh?"

"Funny. Have you, or not?"

His face straightened. "She was coming in pretty regular, but I ain't seen her since they cut the ties." The man nodded toward Brad, then continued. "But, I'll tell ya, she isn't the kind of girl that should be in a dump like this place anyway."

Dana smiled at him; he hadn't seen her. If he had, it seemed he would have been more than happy to tell her, to get the girl out of the place. Adding a nod to her smile, Dana stepped away from the bar.

"Thanks. Will you do me a favor, for her own good? If she stops in, just call me down at the Cozy Cowboy... I'm the owner, Dana. Don't even let her know, just do it."

"Will do."

She left the grimy place sporting a heavy heart and feeling like she needed a shower. It was time to take things to the next level. Dana intended to climb into her car, go back to the Cowboy, and call the police.

She was the one in Andrea Harder's life who cared enough to do it.

That evening, Dana Grulkey placed a call from her office at the Cozy Cowboy to the Cheyenne Police. Much to her dismay, they told her to call back the following day, if Andrea still hadn't 'reared her head,' as they put it. It wouldn't be forty-eight hours until after eleven that night, and that waiting period was policy when the missing person was an adult. She was sure to come around; after all, she was twenty-five and single. Everybody needs to cut loose now and then.

So, Dana sweated each and every remaining minute of Thursday.

CHAPTER 19

Andrea's eyes fluttered open almost as soon as the music went up; it was morning. She easily figured out night from day by the volume of the beautiful music that pumped out of the speakers. Jason lowered it at night when he went to bed, and first thing when he rose, he turned it up. She wasn't sure how many days she had missed, or what day it had been when she woke to find herself here.

She lay in her bed, snug beneath the covers, and gave a long stretch and moan. If she were honest, she would have to say that not having to worry about getting to work, or the walks home at night, were certainly nothing she found herself missing yesterday, and today it sounded even better.

Pulling herself out of bed, Andrea stumbled to the shower, pulling the curtain behind her. She had found a fluffy white bathrobe in the bottom drawer before turning in the night before, and she was looking forward to putting it to use. She started the shower, brushed her teeth, and then jumped into the water.

Andrea took her time. She felt so rested and relaxed. Now, when she thought of Jason, she almost identified with him in a friendly way. Any lingering fears she might have had regarding him doing her harm had been foolishness; the reality was that she could probably punch the guy in the eye and he would do nothing back. He was no threat; that was why he had built the cell for her. That was the only way he could guarantee that she would stay.

No, he had a soft way about him. They had spent the remainder of the evening eating burgers and fries and talking. Jason had even slid a folding chair into her cell so they could sit closer together.

He had talked about his mother, and she had opened up, ever so slightly, about her own. Jason also related some details about his past girlfriends, and the ways they did him wrong. She told him about her first and then left it at that. They also talked about the ranch; she found herself wishing she could see the sheep, and meet Rayne and Winnie, but she never voiced her longing.

When Jason left her for bed that night, he had taken her folding chair back, and she had given it to him willingly.

Now, here she was, standing in the shower thinking of these things, and she knew that something was happening. She was beginning to feel affection for the off-beat, good-looking man who had been put in a box by the enemy. The guy who didn't want to put his horse down quite yet because he loved her, but he was going to because he had to. The same man who she had watched Brad Nagle pummel in front of the Watering

Hole.

The memory made her eyes burn with tears, and Andrea shook her head hard to make them go away.

She turned off the water, grabbed a towel from where it sat on the sink, then wrapped her hair. Stepping out, she wrapped the big robe around her body and moaned... heaven! Now to pick out something to wear.

Going through the clothing that he had purchased for her, Andrea couldn't help but be impressed with his taste. He had done a very good job, especially for a guy. She could never have afforded some of the things he had bought! The best part was that the items seemed to be in line with her taste: jeans and tops, with hoodies here and there.

Soon, she was fully dressed, humming along to a piece from 'Swan Lake,' but she had no idea of its origin; it simply sounded beautiful to her. When had that happened, anyway? Was it getting into her brain while she was sleeping and taking over her mind? Andrea laughed out loud; she was in a strangely wonderful mood, and it made no sense at all.

Giving herself one final look in the mirror after brushing her hair, she found herself longing to have some light makeup. She didn't want to ask, though. Why did she care, anyway? It wasn't normal to want to be attractive in the presence of your captor!

But she didn't feel like it was wrong; he had done absolutely nothing to hurt her, and now she looked forward to breakfast with him.

Seconds later, the music lowered slightly, and the sound of the basement door echoed through the open space. Andrea rushed out from behind the bathroom curtain and walked quickly to the bars. Jason rounded the corner just then with a broad smile.

"Good morning, Lady! Western omelets and toast?"

Andrea beamed. "I could hardly wait!"

∞

Dana was sitting in her office at 8:30, Friday morning, waiting for the officers to come to take her report. They warned her it might take some time until they arrived, so she called in another girl on her day off to cover the still-missing Andrea's shift.

They didn't arrive until ten, and Dana was beside herself. Once they got there, she got the same feeling from the officer on the phone: she'll be here, just wait. They did take the report, and they also took Brad Nagle's name, as well as the names of the Gravitzes. But when they left, they basically offered her condescending condolences and little hope of help.

Something was wrong, she just knew it! She was so convinced of this that her appetite had left her and she hadn't slept a wink. Andrea just didn't run off and party! She was an ambitious young lady who pulled constant doubles, and she lived well for a server because she worked hard. Dana wasn't buying the hogwash from the cops, and she wasn't going to wait around for them to act. She just didn't know what step to take next.

Panic rose up in her throat; she had to think of something. For now, however, it was best that Dana check on the dining room and do what she had to do for now. The first break she got, she would drive down to Andrea's again. In the meantime, she would wait for some kind of break.

CHAPTER 20

Andrea sat on her folding chair by the bars, waiting anxiously for the sound of the music going off. It would not only be the first time in days, but it would also be for a reason she was excited about. Jason asked her if she wanted to watch a movie with him, with popcorn and the works. She would still be in the cell, and he would sit on the other side of the bars, like usual, but they would be hanging out, laughing.

The entire day had been amazing, from the moment she opened her eyes. They had talked, joked, and played a marathon game of Monopoly; she had kicked his keister good, by the way. He had also brought down cleaning supplies and a broom and wet mop. He cleaned his space, and she cleaned hers. While they worked, he told her what each and every sonnet and requiem was, and about the genius who had written it. They also discussed good old rock and roll, a genre they both loved.

It had been superb, and Andrea was smitten.

She had been tempted to act on it. Not in a big way, but more by a casual brush against the arm through the bars or something. Each time she had chickened out.

What if he caught on to her feelings? Then he would change; once they had you, they always changed.

Suddenly, the music stopped; the basement door opened and her heart skipped a beat. It was time! She found herself wondering what movie he had chosen; she hadn't enjoyed a movie in quite a while!

"Okay, all right," came Jason's voice before he even turned the corner. "We have popcorn, we have candy, and we have some soda, of course! Step right up, step right up! Oh, yes, it's Theatre Brandtley!"

Andrea laughed aloud and resisted the urge to clap her hands together like a child. "I love candy!" she shouted.

Jason stopped dead, winked at her, and whispered, "Me too."

He put the tray he was carrying on the bar and pulled a rectangular folding table from behind the bar. Jason sat it up in front of the bars, then put all of the goodies from the tray on it: a massive bowl of buttered popcorn, and the other delights he had promised in large bags. Returning to the bar, he grabbed two cold sodas from the fridge, took one to her, and then plopped down in his own folding chair with the movie in hand.

He spoke in a deep, fancy voice. "For tonight's viewing pleasure, we have the comedy…"

Andrea watched and listened to him fondly as she opened her soda and took a drink. How had she missed all of him before? His beauty, inside and out, was so obvious to her now!

"How do you like the choices, my dear?"

Andrea's eyelashes involuntarily fluttered, and she could feel herself blushing as a result. Jason caught it, and her reaction sent a chill down his body.

"Oh! I almost forgot one thing. I'll be right back!"

Jason jumped up, stopping at the large set on the wall to insert the DVD. "Hey," he said over his shoulder. "Will you please start it? The remote's right there on the table; I can miss the previews."

He winked again, and it took her breath away. With trembling hands and perma-grin, Andrea pressed play, then took another drink. She felt like a schoolgirl.

When Jason returned, she heard his steps stop just around the corner. "Close your eyes, Andrea Harder!"

"What? Why?"

She heard him stifling a laugh.

"Close your eyes, Andrea Harder!"

"Okay, okay! They're closed."

Jason walked around the corner trying to keep Millie under control in his arms. "Open them…"

Andrea opened her eyes, and the little dog was the first thing she saw.

"Millie!"

Andrea jumped up, and Jason put the little dog to the floor. Millie ran toward her and easily slipped through the wide spaces between the bars. Andrea picked her up and buried her face in the clean and freshly groomed dog's coat. She had tears running down her face.

"Oh, my, Jason, you've taken such good care of

her!" Andrea couldn't believe her eyes. The little Yorkie was sporting a bow in her hair and a lacy pink matching collar around her neck. Even her little fingernails were painted. "Jason. You'd be an amazing father."

When he didn't respond, Andrea looked up to see him with a faraway look in his eyes. He was smiling, but his eyes were sad. She realized, all at once, that the handsome, fun-loving man standing there had given up hope for that ever happening for him. He was surviving on his own, alone in his mind, in his own cell. His own cage…

"Thank you, Jason," she said softly. "You're just… amazing. Guess what? I wanted to tell you that, if tomorrow is Saturday, and my calculations are correct, then my birthday is tomorrow; I'll be twenty-six. This is the best gift ever, even if she is my own."

The sound of her beautiful voice brought him to reality. Her twenty-sixth birthday! His mind immediately began planning; he was going to go all out. It was going to be special, something she would remember him for forever!

He snapped out of it and rushed to his folding chair, not wanting to give his thoughts away. Jason began to fast-forward through the previews like an eager kid, but all the while he was daydreaming of the next day, Saturday, the day he would make her feel like a princess.

Then, on Sunday morning, when she woke, she would wake a free woman.

But for now, it was Friday night, and they were together. With Millie, the pair spent the next four hours having the best time of their lives. It was like they were in the company of someone who fully accepted them both; they were in the company of each other.

For Jason, it was right that it hurt...

∞

Dana Grulkey sat at her desk with her head in her hands. She was grieved to the core; here it was, nearly closing time on Friday night, and there hadn't been hide nor hair of Andrea. Dana felt like she had been the one to misplace the girl, and she was wracked with guilt.

A slight knock came at her office door. "Yes?"

"It's Renee. I'm ready to cash out, boss."

Dana bid her entry, and the older server came in and plopped down in one of the chairs across from her. "My feet are killing me. I swear those corn removers just don't do the trick like they used to. It's a scam, I tell you."

Dana chuckled as she entered Renee's receipts into the adding machine and figured her tips. Renee had a shoe off and was rubbing her soles. Dana tried to keep the stale smell out of her nose and say nothing; she knew how the feet felt after twelve hours of running on them.

Suddenly, Renee said out of the blue, "You know, a funny thing crossed my mind today. Remember that guy that came in here... that one that brought Andrea flowers a few weeks back? Remember how she yelled at him like a banshee? You know, it seems to me she said something more about him, but for the life of me..."

Dana held up her hand to stop the server. "Yes! He

sent flowers here! She had the day off!" Renee's tips were now forgotten; Dana's mind was swirling with new thoughts and a flood of realizations.

"Well, what if that guy knows where she is?" Renee uttered conspiratorially. "What if she's with him in some love nest of his?"

Dana sat back hard in her chair, her mouth agape. What if? What if this guy was with Andrea? If Andrea was willing, Dana believed whole-heartedly that she would have called. But what if the reason she hadn't was that the stranger with the flowers was keeping her from it?

CHAPTER 21

"Rise and shine, Beautiful! Happy Birthday!"

Andrea's smile hit her face before she even opened her eyes. She sat up, stretched out, and padded across the carpet in her sweats, her hair tousled. Jason laughed fondly; she was so cute.

"I made you chocolate chip pancakes with strawberry syrup, scrambled eggs coming out of your eyes, and two kinds of meat: sausage and bacon. Eat all you want, I'll make more!"

Andrea giggled as Jason put the tray on the long table. He had left it out, along with the chairs, when he retired late the night before. The thought of trying to make a weapon out of the chair hadn't crossed her mind once. She had gone to bed happy and content.

"Dig in!" Jason said as he handed her a plate. "So, here's my plan for the birthday girl; are you interested?'

She smiled broadly. "Yes."

She heaped eggs on her plate when suddenly he stopped her. Jason handed Andrea silverware rolled into a napkin. "It's the least I can do; don't stab me, okay?"

She stuck her tongue out, and he continued. "So, I have your first gift, which I brought home early this morning, before this, of course. I will bring it down after you eat so you don't get food on it. So, chop, chop!"

Andrea felt like a kid. She could hardly eat because her smile was so wide, and she kept dribbling bits of egg due to it as well. Jason was pacing around, talking about how much he hoped she'd like her gift, and how surprised she would be by the evening he had planned. He had her so excited that she polished off her food in no time with a burp and a belly rub.

"Good one!" he remarked in an impressed voice.

"Okay, Mr. Brandtley," she said, standing. "I'm going to wash my hands, so let's do it! I can't wait!"

Within minutes, she was sitting in her chair waiting for him. She looked around at the left-over food, and suddenly, her eyes saw her silverware. Her knife, fork, and spoon sat there, glistening in the light. Andrea shook her head; there was no way she could ever hurt him now.

When she heard him coming, Andrea jumped up with excitement. Jason rounded the corner, and in his arms, on a fancy hanger, was the most beautiful spring dress she had ever seen! It was formal enough to go out in, yet light enough to wear on a warm spring day. She had never seen anything like the beautiful lace or subtle pattern.

"J-J-Jason," she mumbled, stunned. "It's perfect."

He handed it to her through the bars, beaming. "And this…"

Next came the box. It was perfectly square and

about two inches deep; it appeared to be covered in white leather with a gold design. Andrea couldn't breathe. She carefully laid the dress out on the bed and took the box, her hands shaking like mad. Slowly, she flipped the tiny gold clasp and opened the lid. Nestled inside on black velvet was an incredibly breathtaking pearl necklace with matching earrings. The earrings had two tiny diamonds each. Andrea was shocked beyond words, and tears came to her eyes. She had only daydreamed about things like this.

"Oh, Jason…"

"Hold up." His hand went into the air in his signature move. "And these."

Next, he held a plastic grocery bag through the bars. As she looked inside to discover brand new makeup, Jason spoke.

"I don't know if I got your colors right; it's hard for a man. Now, don't say a word. At four o'clock this evening, I will call on you, and we shall dance to the finest music, and we shall drink the finest wine, and we shall talk until the dawn."

He turned around and abruptly left the room. Andrea just stared after him, her mouth open and tears running down her face. Suddenly, his head popped around the corner, and he said.

"Oh, but I shall bring your luncheon at noon. Perhaps we could play some cards."

With that, Jason was gone.

They ate a simple lunch together of grilled chicken salad sandwiches and tomato soup while Millie played like crazy with a squeaky toy. Jason had brought the dog's bed down right before lunch. Andrea was shocked at how taken the dog was with the overstuffed cushion.

Without discussing the 'dance' at all, they played a couple of games of gin rummy after Jason cleared the dishes. Andrea lost both games; she was so preoccupied with his every word and action that it was as if nothing else existed. She had given up on all thoughts of her apartment or the Cozy Cowboy; it seemed that all she wanted in the world was right in front of her.

On the other side of the bars.

Jason's heart told him that something had changed. His mind longed to hope she felt affection for him, but his doubt and lack of confidence argued it as foolishness. He had made the right decision; he must set the songbird free. The time they had spent together had changed his entire opinion of her. Andrea was not the rude girl he had met before; she was a mature, polite, intelligent woman, and he would miss her terribly.

At quarter-to-three, Jason dismissed himself from her presence, but not before folding up the table and putting it away. He also surprised her by pulling a second recliner out from around the corner, just out of her sight. They would have their fine wine there!

So, she got ready, a sense of sadness in her heart because Andrea was also aware that her time here was drawing to a close.

Jason and Andrea danced.

In each other's arms, to the lulling sounds of Bach, Beethoven, and the requiems of the caged. They laughed as they danced, and they talked. They both gave up everything that night; they bared their mutual souls and shared burdens with one another. Both of them managed to cry, for reasons both obvious and unspoken.

Both of them felt grief, but nothing was said about it. So caught up in every moment together were they that they didn't want to spoil it. She gushed about the white tux he wore and the way he wore his cowboy boots with it. He stared at her as if she was the most beautiful woman on Earth.

Then, it was midnight.

Much like in Cinderella's fairy tale, it was time to say goodnight; he made it clear.

They got to the door of the cell. Andrea entered, then turned around and met his eyes. She was a vision.

Suddenly, she took two steps forward in her bare feet, stood on her toes, and kissed him.

It was a wonderful kiss, a perfect kiss, the kind of kiss she'd always dreamed of. Her arms went around his neck, and she concentrated only on the softness of his lips and the scent of his clean skin. He tasted sweet and good, and she knew that was because he was sweet and good.

Jason began to pull away, to resist the embrace they had held. She tasted like candy, the touch of her skin sent chills down his spine. "Happy Birthday, Andrea." He looked her in the eyes, winked, and stepped back to close the door. "Sweet dreams. You are beautiful and worthy of a happy life."

Then Jason was gone.

Andrea cried herself to sleep that night because she knew what the morning held.

CHAPTER 22

Andrea woke to a breeze on her face.

Her eyes fluttered open, and she looked around. The cell door was wide open. The master she had come to know as Mozart drifted from the speakers and a section of wall over the bar had been removed. A large, open window was now there, near the ceiling. It was wide open, and the smells of Jason's ranch drifted through pleasantly. Millie was nowhere in sight.

She stood up and walked out of the cell slowly, noting that she was wearing her dress from the night before. It didn't matter now; what mattered was to find Jason. She wouldn't leave him; he couldn't make her. She had to find him and tell him she loved him before it was too late.

Andrea crossed Jason's part of the basement and timidly rounded the corner. A steep set of carpeted stairs leading upward ended at an open door. The thought of going through it made her sick to her stomach; she couldn't bear it.

"Jason!"

He didn't answer, so she took the steps two-at-a-time until she reached the top, nearly tripping on the hem of her dress more than once.

"Jason! Jason!"

A huge kitchen with skylight windows loomed before her, spotless and orderly. On the other side of that, through yet another door, was a dining room with what looked to be some of the finest oak furniture on the planet. She was struck by the beauty of the home's aesthetic, but she didn't let it stop her. She passed through the kitchen and dining room. The next room appeared to be a living area. The door was wide open, and a beautiful breeze blew through it, into the entire house.

Televisions and stereo parts were set up tastefully to the right, next to a large flagstone fireplace. A closed door was next, followed by the main, open door. To the right was all of the furnishings.

Jason was on the couch.

He was sitting up, petting Millie; she was relaxed and happy on his lap. He was pale, and his eyes were swollen from crying. Jason looked like he hadn't slept a wink.

∞

With a quick call to Fancy Florists, Dana was able to get Jason Brandtley's name and address in Chesterfield. According to the guy at the market, the drive to Brandtley Ranch wasn't too far ahead. She had just left the town of Chesterfield, as she sped up the highway towards Brandtley Ranch. Dana had no idea if she would find Andrea there, but she had to try because the cops weren't going to do anything. She had given them the information, and they had told her that Jason Brandtley was a good young man from a fine family. They said if Andrea were smart, she'd stay right where she was. Dana decided to visit the ranch herself.

Suddenly, almost too fast, she came upon the gravel turn off. She hung a sharp right, righted the car from a swerve, and started up the road.

∞

"I will not leave, Jason; you can't send me away now." Andrea was nearly sobbing.

Jason stood up and took her into his arms just as Dana pulled up in front of the house. "What are you saying, Andrea?" Jason replied.

Dana saw Andrea right away, standing in the guy's arms in the middle of the living room. She had a clear view through that massive front door. My, it was a big house!

Dana ran up the front walk and to the open door. "Andrea! I've been worried sick!"

Andrea took her face from Jason's tear-covered chest, but her embrace tightened. "Dana? What are you doing here?"

Dana's mouth dropped open. "Are you kidding me, kid?"

Andrea chuckled and wiped at her eyes. "I guess I should have called you." She gave a laugh. "Jason here has been giving me a bit of therapy. Today is my graduation day."

With a sad smile, Jason kissed her lips softly and said, "I love you, Andrea Harder. Don't forget me when you go back to the big city."

Andrea gazed at him, turned to Dana, then said, "I won't be going anywhere, Dana. I'm so sorry.

"But I think I've finally come home…"

ENTREATY

This book was made possible by reviews from readers like you. Reviews fuel my creativity. If you enjoyed this novel, I implore you to please write a review and share your experience on the retailer's website. The livelihood for authors is entirely dependent on reviews, and I must say, it is the largest obstacle as a struggling author that I have encountered. Please tell a friend, tell a loved one about this read. With your help, I will be one step closer to overcoming this obstacle. In return, I thank you from the bottom of my heart, and sincerely appreciate your time and effort.

Humbled, with gratitude,

R.W.K. Clark

ABOUT THE AUTHOR

I am a father of two beautiful children, Jon and Kim. They are my motivating forces; they are the lighthouse in this vast ocean. In my life, they are the air that I breathe; they are the oasis in this desert of uncertainty. They are my greatest joy in life and my number one priority. I have a long list of hobbies, and I attribute that to my lust for life! I like to surround myself with positive people, who share the same interests. Family values, the arts, outdoors, nature, and travel are tops on my list. I embrace attending cultural and artistic events because I believe dramatic self-expression is the window to the soul. I wear my heart on my sleeve, and I still believe in chivalry, and I always treat people the way I want to be treated.

www.rwkclark.com